SCHOOL
SHENANIGANS
5
by CarolinaKidd
Illustration: by LeRoy Grayson
Publishing: by Jazzy Kitty Publications

School Shenanigans

By Isaac Brown Jr. "CarolinaKidd"

Cover Art Created by LeRoy Grayson

Logo Design by Justin Ackerman and Angel Jones

Editor: Anelda Attaway

DEDICATIONS

March 26, 1963- April 9, 1963. This book is dedicated to my Aunt Shelia Ann. Your time was short-lived, but you will never be forgotten. I never got a chance to meet her, but I know we would've laughed, loved, and cried together.

RIP Auntie

ACKNOWLEDGMENTS

First and foremost, I want to acknowledge the Lord Jesus Christ. He is my everything. My inspiration and motivation. Because of him, there was no need for hesitation on the way to my destination. Amen!

Next, I would like to acknowledge any non-believer of Christ. The Bible says in Romans 10:8, 9, 10 that if you confess with your mouth "Jesus is Lord" and believe in your heart that he died and was risen again on the third day, then you shall be saved. Amen! Amen!

Lastly, I would like to acknowledge the late great Tammy Wiggins Brown. RIP Mommy. There isn't a day that goes by that I don't think about you. You departed from me on August 5, 2008, at 3:05 p.m. I remember it like it was yesterday. And even though your physical presence has been long gone, I see your light shine bright through your 3 handsome grandboys. I see your attitude in Isaiah, your smile in Joseph, and your stubbornness in Kyng. I loved you before I could even begin to know what love was because you set forth such an empowering and nurturing example that I must carry on down the line to not just my children but any young mind that I can mold in a positive way.

Thanks Ma.

TABLE OF CONTENTS

INTRODUCTION

If they'll fit, place yourself in the shoes of a young man faced with everyday choices. From simple to complicated decisions, Jerry must learn to navigate through school and life in general. Like many of us, Jerry was provided with a plethora of positive and negative influences, but it is up to him not to fall into temptation. Jerry is very self-aware yet lacks accountability from time to time. He has a slight temper problem that stems from a traumatizing moment that happened a few years back, but he still has a big heart. He doesn't fear anything or anyone. His emotions get the best of him sometimes, but follow along and find out how he learns to control those emotions, stay focused, and think more logically.

CHAPTER 1

JERRY'S WORLD

"Jerry! Jerry!! Jerry!!!"

"What?" Jerry replied with an aggravated look on his face.

"Class has started, but you haven't," said Mr. Reid, "everyone has started their work, yet you have not; different day, same Jerry," as he shakes his head.

"Well, Mr. Reid, I've always been known to be a trendsetter, not too much of a follower," Jerry said sarcastically, "something like an Omega wolf." As the class outbursts with laughter, Mr. Reid's response was intellectual as always.

"You know Jerry, in order to be a great leader or trendsetter as you say, you must first learn to follow and take orders. Without it being done in that order, you will just be blind while leading the blind right off a cliff."

"Great point Mr. Reid, but I never said I was leading anyone to the promised land." The class erupted with laughter again.

"Jerry, just do your work. You somehow always have enough energy to go back and forth with me but never enough energy to complete an assignment put before you. How ironic."

As funny and attention-grabbing as Jerry was, he was also known as a fighter. He was only in the 7th grade, but he averaged about two fights a year since the 3rd grade. He was such a sweet child from preschool to 2nd grade, but there was a series of events that caused his behavior to take a turn for the worst.

Jerry's father, Jerry Sr., was Jerry's biggest role model, his hero, and the only male figure in his life. His dad would take him fishing, out for ice cream, watch and play any sport imaginable, and he was funny. Jerry Sr. never put up with nonsense or disrespect from Jerry Jr., and he was big on education. To Jerry Jr., his dad was perfect, without flaw, but one day, something happened that replayed in Jerry's head over and over again. It was an average Saturday afternoon and Jerry was fully dressed for another fishing trip with his dad. He had just loaded the back of his dad's truck with fishing rods, the tackle box, and snacks and drinks. He was overwhelmed with joy just to be with his dad. It really had nothing to do with fishing; it was all about the time spent, but as he was loading the truck, he heard his parents arguing back and forth. It was normal to hear them fuss, but this time it did seem to be a lot louder than usual.

When his father finally came out of the room, Jerry Jr. ran to the passenger seat, yelling, "Hurry up Pop! Those fish ain't gonna catch themselves!" Jerry Sr. smirked with his eyes full of water.

He hopped in the truck, told Jerry how much he loved him, and then cranked up. Before they pulled off, he asked Jerry to run in the house and grab his six-pack of beer out of the refrigerator. Jerry sprinted as fast as he could, but by the time he got back to the door, all he could see was the taillights and license plate on the back of his dad's truck. Jerry never saw his dad again after that day, but the moment lasted forever. To this day, Jerry thinks of that moment, and it starts to make his emotions uncontrollable. When he cries, he weeps; when he laughs, he cries, and his anger turns to hate. He releases his frustration out onto others who have nothing to do with his situation; they just happen to be in his line of fire. He has been spoken to many times about his anger. From instructors to administration, friends, and family, and his own conscience even knows he gets out of character at times. He tries to talk himself down by counting to ten frontwards and back. He even keeps a pop-it on him at all times to help relieve stress and to help him not fidget as much.

The bell has rang, and as usual, Jerry drags as slowly as possible into his next class. Miss Joyner is already shaking her head and rolling her eyes at the fact of Jerry coming in late.

"Jerry!" Miss Joyner says, "why must you be late to my class every day? I mean, at this point, do you think you could even be on time for your own funeral?" Jerry thinks about what she says for a second and begins to chuckle.

"That was a good one, Miss Joyner. I know I be late, but you are my favorite teacher."

"Am late, Jerry and Oh Wow! I could imagine being your least favorite," said Miss Joyner, "have a seat and join the rest of the class."

Miss Joyner taught History, which was Jerry's favorite subject. He enjoyed hearing about previous wars and their strategies to triumph or overcome. He was intrigued by great leaders, kings, and emperors on how they ran their empires throughout history. Jerry always wondered where he would fit in back in those times. He would ask himself things like, *would he be just another amongst the common, maybe an outcast, or would he be a prince groomed to one day be king?* He even thought of being a slave, servant, or prisoner of the king and the many different ways he would try to escape. Jerry is a very bright student, even though, at times, it may not show through his actions or reflect on his report card.

Jerry was only lacking a little structure combined with discipline. He would soon run into the correct resources he needed in order to get himself going on the right track.

Well, history class has now ended, and it's time for lunch. Jerry never knew what mystery meat or mystery treat was being served, but whatever it was, Jerry knew he was getting his portion. On the way to the cafeteria, he would hear other kids make fun of school lunch, trash talk school lunch, and usually, once they sat down for lunch, someone would throw school lunch or dispose of school lunch with no care in the world. Jerry would never disrespect a free meal. He understood that his home life situation wasn't the most fortunate and that moments like this, when he is able to take advantage of something free, is called a blessing and an opportunity. He would even talk to some of the other students who didn't want their lunch to still get in line so that he could eat theirs as well. He figured, since they were going to make waste of it anyway, why not? Jerry enters the cafeteria rubbing his hands together, smiling from ear to ear, nostrils flared wide open, awaiting the aroma to come rushing up his nose, straight to his brain to only imagine what it could be. All of a sudden, Dillon, a classmate standing in front of him, farts silently as Jerry was sniffing as hard as he could. Jerry's face begins to turn sour, and Dillon is doing all he can to hold back the laughter.

"Oh God!!!" Jerry said, "what is that smell?" Dillon couldn't take it anymore; he burst out with laughter.

"My bad Bro," Dillon said with water in his eyes, "my stomach has been bubbling since this morning. My momma fed me some beans for breakfast."

"Now she ought to be ashamed of herself for setting you up like that," Jerry said, laughing as the smell started to fade away.

"Bro, that really stinks. You gotta warn somebody next time," Jerry said, "you almost damaged my sense of smell." They both burst out again with laughter.

"Quiet! Quiet! Close your mouths!!!" Mrs. Fleming yelled as silence fell over the lunchroom.

"Now we go through this every day; this isn't nothing new. You are to be quiet in line as you wait for your food, and once you are seated, then you may talk quietly amongst the ones around you. Grab everything you need before you take a seat because once you are seated, you are not to get up. If there is anyone who does not understand these simple orders, you may come join me and have a silent lunch as you watch your peers model these instructions."

Jerry smacks his lips and mumbles something sarcastic under his breath, then Dillon snickers at what was said. It seemed as if Mrs. Fleming's hearing was as good as a gazelle eating out of high grass in an open field.

"Jerry, since you and Dillon are choosing to talk now, after y'all grab your lunch, come and join me for a silent lunch until your class leaves. Have a good day, everyone continue on."

Jerry was so mad he could spit. His fist was clenched, sweating all over and staring directly at Mrs. Fleming. It wasn't that she gave him silent lunch; it was how she did it. He felt so embarrassed about how she called him out in front of the whole cafeteria. Jerry doesn't really like to take accountability for his own decisions. He really can't see where he is wrong in too many situations. Either that, or he felt like they had it coming, almost like they deserved what he did to them. Mrs. Fleming was a target for Jerry. This silent lunch is most definitely not their first encounter.

As Jerry grabs his lunch, Dillon shoves him a little and says, "Every time I'm around you, I get in trouble; you are no good Jerry. I wish you didn't even go to this school."

Jerry shoves him back, "Shut up Dillon, you disrespected my nose with yo stanking…"

"Cut it out, fellas," Mrs. Fleming said, "before y'all spend the rest of the day in ISS." Dillon just shakes his head and takes a seat. Jerry thinks to himself about how good Mrs. Fleming's hearing is.

"Have a seat Jerry!" Mrs. Fleming said sternly.

"I am! Dang!" Jerry said, aggravated.

"Excuse me, young man!"

"Nothing, nothing, Mrs. Fleming."

"That's what I thought. Have a seat." Jerry rolls his eyes and flops down in the seat.

"Jerry, let's not do this today," said Mrs. Fleming, "just look at this silent lunch as time for you to get yourself together so that you can finish having a productive day."

Jerry wouldn't say a word. He heard everything she said but acted as if he didn't. Lunch was only about 20 to 25 minutes long, so Jerry was disgusted and had lost his appetite for about the first 10 minutes of lunch. Like I said that only lasted about 10 minutes because square pepperoni pizza and tater tots were on the menu for lunch. As his mouth began to water from the smell of that delicious pizza, his stomach began to growl to the point of pain because he had not eaten breakfast that morning. He overslept, missed the bus, and his mother overslept and was almost late for work. She only had enough time to drop him off and just barely made it to work on time. Her boss had already spoken with her on two separate occasions, so she wasn't looking for a strike three. Even though she woke up late, she still fussed at Jerry for missing the bus.

"I've told you time after time about staying up late on that phone and on that game. It causes you to run behind on your responsibilities. You have so much potential, yet you choose to put your energy into things you will get nothing out of in the long run. Son, I know I'm not perfect, and there are so many ways that I can be an even better example for you in life, but I really want you to understand that I am trying and I will never give up on trying to succeed as long as there is breath in my body," his Mom said with so much passion in her voice, "and that's one of the main things I want to instill in you Son. **The will to keep going on, pressing, and fighting, even through rough times, become tougher than tough times. Stand strong!"**

Jerry pondered on the things his mom shared with him that morning as he ate quietly. He also thought about what was coming up next after lunch. Elective time!!! Today's elective is Physical Education, better known as P.E., so he felt he had something to look forward to after that trainwreck of a lunch session. As Jerry was finishing his lunch, which wasn't taking long at all, he saw his class walking in a straight line quietly, headed to throw their trays away.

"Mrs. Fleming, my class is leaving," he said.

"I can see that Jerry," said Mrs. Fleming.

"You and Dillon grab your trays, get in the back of the line, and remember, have a productive rest of your day."

Jerry couldn't get out of that seat fast enough. He nearly tripped over his own feet, trying to break away so swiftly. On the other hand, Dillon was dragging and still upset about serving silent lunch. He had only eaten half his food because he let it get too cold, thinking about the trouble he had gotten himself into messing around with Jerry. Plus, those beans hadn't quite settled down in his stomach yet, either. As Jerry was following his class out of the cafeteria, he noticed he was behind his class crush.

"Hey Stacy," Jerry said.

"Shhh, Jerry, we're not supposed to talk in line," Stacy whispered, "you're gonna get us in trouble."

Stacy was a goodie-two-shoes type of girl. She never caused any problems and her grades were always the best. Stacy was dark-skinned, with long black hair, but in the sun, it looked as if it was sandy brown. She had thick, full lips that were moisturized at all times. Also, she was fluffy but curvy with the cutest bifocals, which is what really had Jerry's attention. He didn't really know how to talk to a girl. His only practice had come from TV lines he would quote in the mirror to his imaginary girlfriend or from his many pillows with different names every night. So, with that being said, a lot of times, he would just stare and become very creative in his thought process. As they headed to electives, Jerry would do any and everything to get Stacy's attention. He would kick her, try to trip her, tap her shoulder, pull her hair, repeat her name, etc. She knew Jerry liked her, and even though he was annoying and known to be a troublemaker, she thought it was cute how he was always wanting her attention, and she liked the fact that he would stick up or take the blame for her. Just the other day in class, Stacy forgot to put her phone on vibrate and once it went off, she quickly silenced it, but the teacher still heard the device and wanted to know who the culprit was. Jerry saw the fear in Stacy's eyes, so he quickly took the blame and just gave up his phone until the end of the day. Stacy never forgot that moment; it always did mark down some cool points for Jerry in her book. She never got a chance to thank Jerry, but she figured today in P.E. would be the perfect time to bring it up if only he would stop being so annoying at the time.

"Class, today we will get stretched out, run, jog, and or walk so that we can get our blood flowing," said Mr. Perry, "then after that, we will head outside into this warm weather and get us a friendly, competitive game of kickball going out on the baseball field."

"Aww man! This sucks!" The lazy kids complained.

"It's too hot! The gnats are bad! And the grass is too high!" The girls complained.

"I wanted to play basketball! Mr. Perry, I thought today was soccer day. I'm cool with outside!" Some of the boys shouted.

Even with demands all over the place, Mr. Perry was not intimidated by the angry child mob. With a smooth, calm voice, Mr. Perry said with a smile on his face, "I hear and empathize with all of your differences, but after deep thought and consideration, kickball is still the deciding factor. For those who do not wish to participate, know that it does affect your grade. Now, y'all know the drill in your lines so that we may begin stretching."

As they began their stretching, Jerry would make sure he positioned himself so that he could watch Stacy as she stretched. Jerry didn't think she knew he was watching, but she did. There are a few instances where Stacy would look back, catching eye contact with Jerry, but he would look away quickly as if he weren't mesmerized. Jerry was absolutely intrigued by Stacy. He loved everything about her; her laugh, her sneeze, the way she would wiggle her fingers as her hand waved in the air, and waiting on the edge of her seat to be called on. Her eyes, her pretty colored nails and feet, and whatever else there was to love about her, he did.

While Mr. Perry was picking teams for kickball, Jerry hoped and prayed he and Stacy would be on the same team. Secretly, so was Stacy, but Jerry wanted it more. Unfortunately, they did not end up on the same team, which really bummed Jerry. He was looking for his chance to just sit beside Stacy in the dugout, but as the game went on, he got out of his feelings and had the most fun possible while playing kickball. Jerry was drenched in sweat when the game ended, with a slight odor coming from under his armpits.

As they got in line and headed toward the locker room to change, Tina, one of Jerry's classmates, said, "Jerry, is that you that smells that way?"

"I don't know," Jerry says as he smells himself, "check your top lip; that could be where the smell is coming from."

"Shut up Jerry," Tina said angrily, "you're always joking, but I'm serious, you stink." Stacy overheard Jerry and Tina arguing.

"Girl don't let Jerry get under your skin, you know how he is," Stacy whispered to Tina, "you know he's silly and ain't got no sense."

Both girls started laughing with each other as they entered the locker room. Jerry wondered what was said as he was dressing back out for class. He thought to himself *that maybe Stacy was in agreement with Tina.* Jerry could smell himself without lifting his armpits, so he knew he had an odor. For the moment, Jerry was embarrassed and he felt he had to do something quick. He remembered some of the things his mom shared with him about hygiene and one of those things was, you can't put fragrance on top of funk. What she meant by that is you have to bathe first before you put on any cologne or deodorant. Now this particular locker room didn't have an area for Jerry to bathe, so he had to improvise and improvise fast before the bell rang and the last class of the day began. He glanced at the sink and noticed the soap dispenser above. As the rest of the boys were leaving, Jerry headed straight to the sink, turning on the freezing cold water, splashing himself under his armpits back and forth.

As the chill bumps ran down his spine from the temp of the water, he said to himself out loud, *"Why doesn't the hot water side ever work, like, I turn the knob and water won't even come out."*

"Jerry, who are you talking to?" Mr. Perry says as he enters the locker room.

"Nobody Mr. Perry, I like to talk to myself at times, he never interrupts me."

Mr. Perry chuckled and said, "Well hurry up Jerry or you'll get left behind. Your class is already moving and oh yeah, check the locker by the stall, on the bottom shelf, and you will see what you need."

As Mr. Perry exited the locker room, Jerry tapped the soap dispenser repetitively as fast as he could and scrubbed under both his armpits and chest. Then he began to splash water on himself again in order to get the soap off, but that didn't go exactly as planned. It took a little more time than he thought, but at least he smelled fresh now. He hurried to put his shirt on and grab his bag to head out the locker room, but as soon as he opened the door he realized he forgot to check the locker by the stall. He quickly ran to open it and squatted down to observe the bottom shelf. On that shelf, he discovered a few sticks of deodorant and two cans of AXE body spray. Exactly what the doctor ordered for Jerry, he was excited and thankful. He gave himself about two or three swipes under each armpit and two good sprays of AXE. Jerry was feeling like a new man, so he stuck his chest out and walked like one with his head up and a smile on the way to his next class.

CHAPTER 2

SCHOOL'S OUT

Yes, Jerry was late to his final class of the day, but he felt it was necessary so that he wouldn't get joked on by anyone else in the class, especially Stacy. When he finally got to class, the door was already closed and locked. As he peeked through the glass of the wooden door, he saw Miss. Sanchez's finger pointing him in the direction of the office. He already knew what that meant.

"Really Miss. Sanchez! I'm like two minutes late. Is it that serious?"

Miss. Sanchez never even acknowledged Jerry. She just kept on teaching her class and pointing toward the office. Jerry huffed, puffed, and stomped his way to the office. He couldn't believe Miss. Sanchez was making him walk all the way to the office for just a couple of minutes.

"She really be doing too much," Jerry said to himself out loud as he entered the main building, where he was immediately greeted by Mrs. Stevens, the school receptionist.

"Well, hello Jerry!" She said with excitement, "are you talking to yourself again?"

"Hey Mrs. Stevens, yea, you know how I do," Jerry said, nodding his head.

"What can I help you with today Jerry? You weren't tardy again, were you?" Jerry drops his head.

"Yes Ma'am," Jerry said, "but it was only like two minutes!"

"Late is late young man and time is your most valuable asset, so don't waste it," Mrs. Stevens said, firm but loving, like she always does.

"Yes Ma'am, Mrs. Stevens," Jerry said with his head still down.

"Now, what class were you tardy for?"

"Miss. Sanchez," Jerry said begrudgingly.

"And you know she doesn't play," said Mrs. Stevens, "she's gonna write you up every time. She holds y'all accountable, as she should."

She went on and on for a few minutes about how good of a teacher Miss. Sanchez was and how some of the other teachers around the school should model after her methods. Then she sent Jerry back off to class with his tardy pass. Once Jerry approached the wooden door again to Miss. Sanchez's class, he slapped the tardy pass on the glass. Of course, it got everyone's attention.

Miss. Sanchez rushed to the door, "Jerry! Must you always make a grand entrance," she said rhetorically, "you find a way every day to disrupt my class and it's starting to get old Jerry. When are you going to do better?"

"You should've just let me in the first time I came to the door," Jerry said.

"Don't tell me what I should've done young man. Stay in a child's place and have a seat," said Miss. Sanchez.

Jerry rolled his eyes, shook his head, and thought to himself *how much time was left before the bell rang for school to be dismissed*. It was about another 45 minutes or so before school was let out, so in the meantime, Jerry started to feel bored, fatigued, and just plain out uninterested in what Miss. Sanchez was instructing. He gave in to his tiredness and just put his head down on his desk. Falling asleep in class was also one of Jerry's downfalls. There goes the bell, and Jerry sat up alert as if he had been awake the entire time. He packed his things, stood up, and headed straight for the exit.

"The bell doesn't dismiss you, I do!" Miss Sanchez said loudly to the class, "now have a seat, and I will dismiss you in rows. Make sure that you stop by your locker and grab everything you need to take home on the bus."

Jerry was in the last row, so by the time she called his row, he had an attitude. He felt like Miss. Sanchez was purposely starting with the row on the other side of the room just so that he would go last. As Jerry left the room, he looked at Miss. Sanchez with disgust and disbelief, but she also matched his energy with her look of disgust as well.

Once Jerry got on the bus, he saw Stacy and a few of her friends, in the first couple of rows, but Jerry was headed straight for the back. A few of his companions were already back there, ready to embrace him, and talk about their days. To Jerry, a lot of times, this was the highlight of his day. They would beatbox, freestyle, roast, and most importantly, talk about girls.

"I saw you looking at Stacy when you got on the bus Bro. When you gone stop being scared and just ask her to the spring dance?" Tony asked Jerry.

"Bro, I'm not scared," Jerry said, "I'm just waiting on the right timing."

"Yea, yea, you're gonna time yourself out doing all this waiting. Better hurry before someone else takes her," Tony said. Jerry looked back towards the front at Stacy, thinking about what Tony had said.

"Yo Jerry, drop that beat," Tony said.

Jerry was a pretty decent beatboxer. He could make all kinds of crazy sounds with his mouth. No one in the back of the bus could freestyle that well, but it didn't bother them. They would all still take turns jumping in and out the beat like a game of double dutch. Most of the time they would get tongue-tied on their delivery, but every now and then, someone would give you a good eight to 12 bars without interruption. Jerry could freestyle a little, but for the most part, he just made very rare, unique sounds with his mouth. Stacy would always watch Jerry out of her peripheral vision when she heard him beatboxing. She never wanted to look too eager at whatever Jerry was doing.

Jerry had the back of the bus rocking with his beatbox abilities. He had everybody's head nodding, feet tapping, and hands clapping. Before you knew it, the bus had come to a stop and it was time for Jerry, Stacy, and a few other kids to exit the bus.

"Hurry along boys and girls," the bus driver said, "you're holding up traffic."

Stacy and a couple of her friends got off first, and Jerry, who was the only one to get off from the back of the bus, wasn't far behind. As they got off the bus, looking in both directions for traffic, they crossed over the road as fast as they could while the coast was clear. They knew cars had to stop when the bus did, but it was still fun to run across as if it were for their lives. As they walked the dirt path, heading to each of their homes, Jerry would hang back a few steps and practice beatboxing while Stacy and her friends would look back, laughing and snickering. Stacy stayed next door to Jerry, and both of their houses were at the end of the dirt road on the right. After the dirt path was nothing but trees destined to touch the sky, Jerry assumed, because of how tall they were. Stacy waved at Jerry as she was walking up the steps of her house. Her dad was standing in the door with the meanest look on his face, staring at Jerry. Jerry waved back at Stacy cautiously because of her dad's demeanor.

"Bye, Stacy," Jerry said as he began to run towards his house, "see you tomorrow.”

Opening the screen door, Jerry went rushing through the front door like a gust of wind.

“Boy what did I tell you about running in my house!” Shelia Ann said.

Shelia Ann was Jerry’s mom. She was short, so was her hair, she was plump, loud, dark-skinned, and feisty. Her love for Jerry is unconditional and without question. Jerry is her only child. She suffered from two other miscarriages in her past, so Jerry was her golden child, her blessing, her reason to not give up. She cherished him, but she did not spoil him. One thing she could not stand is a spoiled child. She worked hard for what she did have and she would make sure that Jerry understood the definition of hard work, and how to build a strong work ethic.

“Junior!!!” Shelia Ann yelled from the kitchen, “I know you hear me.”

Jerry walks back into the kitchen, “Sorry Ma, I forgot.”

“You forgot! Well, I bet you won’t forget this belt I’m about to glue to your backside,” Shelia Ann said angrily.

“Maaaa! I said I was sorry. I won’t do it anymore, I promise,” Jerry said, fearful but strategically.

He knew his mother didn’t really like to punish him through whooping’s. She would if she felt it was entirely necessary, but for the most, she would just take things and privileges away from him. He also knew if he wined and said he was sorry enough, then she would usually just send him to his room.

“Boy, get out my face and go clean that junkyard you call a room!,” Shelia Ann yelled, “matter of fact, start on that homework first then clean that pigsty of a room!”

"Yes Ma'am," Jerry said as he walked away hastily.

The moment Jerry entered his room, he immediately connected his phone to a little Bluetooth off-brand speaker he had gotten from a yard sale he and his mother just so happened to run into early one Saturday morning. He hated to even get up and go that particular morning, but he was glad he did. That speaker turned out to be one of his most prized possessions. His mother also got him two old fishing rods, but they were still in pretty good shape. While he was doing his homework and cleaning his room, he would throw on his instrumental playlist from YouTube. He enjoyed hearing the mixture of beats, and he would do his best at imitating them. He couldn't wait to get on the bus and let the boys hear a new sound he had down pack. From time to time, while Jerry was cleaning his room and halfway completing his assignments, he would look out of his window over to Stacy's house. Their bedroom windows faced each other. She would pass by the window every now and then, but she would never stand there long enough for Jerry to get a good look, and if she did, the blinds would be drawn and the curtain closed shut.

Once Jerry finished his work, he glanced at the clock and noticed he had about an hour to an hour and a half until dinner time. Dinner wasn't usually ready until around 8 or 8:30 p.m., so he figured he had time to go down by the pond and cast his rod. He would usually catch them and then let them go. He enjoyed the sport of it, but mostly when he fished, it was just time for him to sit and think on the moments he and his dad spent fishing. He had remembered everything his dad taught him about how to catch, clean, and eat a fish. His dad always compared fishing to life. He preached patience and timing when it came to both. He would also tell Jerry that fish bait is something like your dreams, your goals, your imagination and that you are to cast it as far into the world as possible. More than one will bite, but never forget to go back and feed your family. Jerry put on his fishing attire, grabbed his gear, and headed straight for the door without any permission or awareness of where he was going.

"Junior, if you walk out that door, you are sleeping on that side of it this good night," Shelia Ann said.

"Maaa, I'm just going down by the pond to fish," Jerry said.

"Yea, but I haven't checked behind you to see if your room is clean and your homework complete," Shelia Ann emphasized, "plus, you didn't ask me about leaving this house, and that's something you must do every time. I need to know when you are in and when you are out. Understand?"

"Yes Ma'am, I understand," Jerry said.

"Now go on down to the pond, dinner will be ready by 8:30 and I expect you to be sitting down with your hands washed, ready to eat." Jerry took off out the door at full speed, but Shelia Ann wasn't done talking.

She yelled out the screen door, "And if that homework ain't done right and that room is still messy, you are not going back down to that pond for two weeks!"

Jerry heard her but he kept on sprinting. The pond was through the tall trees at the end of the road. There was a dirt path trail that led directly into the pond. Jerry usually stayed the course all the way down to the pond. He wasn't too interested in venturing off into other parts of the woods. He had seen too many movies where it doesn't work out for the guy who's most curious. Being down by the pond was like a vacation for Jerry. It was a getaway from all his school drama. He also enjoyed all the sounds mother nature had to offer. The way the insects buzzed, the way the birds chirp, and the way the fish would splash the water. It was like some sort of therapy for him. At times he would practice imitating the sounds he heard while he was fishing, but he would always look around first before he would do so. He never wanted to be looked at as a weirdo for practicing bug and animal noises. He was just always looking to add another sound to his beatbox collection. He didn't care where the tune came from. If his mouth could make it, he was gone take it.

As Jerry was fishing and beatboxing, he suddenly came to a halt. He had heard a noise and it wasn't the usual sounds he was accustomed to hearing. He felt as if he were hearing footsteps, almost like someone had been watching and following him. He glanced around the woods, but he didn't want to make it seem obvious, so he would just look from side to side out of his peripherals. If he was being followed, he didn't want the stalker to know he was on to them. Jerry knew those woods like the sweaty palms of his hands. He knew that if there was anyone out there ready to attack him, they had better be in shape. Jerry was fast and it seemed as if his endurance had endurance. He never ran out of breath, no matter what activity he was attending. Wild animals were the next thing Jerry thought it could be. First he thought maybe it could be a stray dog, a cat, a possum, or a racoon. Then he started thinking bigger.

"What if it's a bear," Jerry said as he swallows spit, "I gotta get out of here, it's almost time for dinner anyway."

Jerry gathered his things and headed back towards home. As he was walking, he would look back and forth over both shoulders watching his surroundings. Jerry was paranoid and it seemed like he couldn't get home fast enough. At this point, every sound he heard frightened him, he couldn't take it any longer, so he just went ahead and ran on home.

As Jerry was getting closer to home, he could already smell Shelia Ann's homemade honey butter biscuits from outside. His mouth began to water as he walked in. He noticed his mom's famous tea on the counter, full of strawberries and steaming hot with two glasses full of ice beside it. It was labeled famous tea because everyone in the neighborhood knew about it and loved it dearly. As Jerry entered his house, he was still frightened by the thought of being followed, but the sight and smell of his momma food quickly made his fears go away. He drops his things at the door and goes to have a seat.

As soon as he pulls the chair back Shelia Ann says, "Now you know better than to sit at my table before washing your hands and go pick up that stuff you dropped by the door. I'm not your maid, I'm your mother. Have some respect and appreciation for the things I already do and provide for you, and you can do that by cleaning up behind yourself or taking out the trash without being asked. You know, small things, they always add up to the bigger picture."

Jerry quickly did as his mother asked because he was hungry and quite thirsty after that run home. By the time he got back to the dinner table, his plate was hot and ready, and Jerry could see the ice from his glass melting away quickly from the steaming strawberry tea. He sits down, sips his tea, and grabs his fork.

"Say your grace Jerry," Shelia Ann said.

"Oh yea, I almost forgot," Jerry said as he bowed his head, "Amen! Momma, this food smells so good, and I know it tastes even better. You put your feet in this one, huh Ma? All ten toes," Jerry said jokingly, "that's the secret ain't it?"

"Boy, hush, sounding like yo daddy. Looking like him is bad enough, I don't need any extra reminders."

"Ma, when's the last time you heard from pop? What is he doing now? Where is he at?"

"Those are too many questions for one day Son, just know that your father is living his best life," Shelia Ann said, as she finished up washing the dirty dishes.

"What? His best life," Jerry said confusingly.

"Yes, his best life, but don't worry about that right now. How was your day?"

Jerry takes a few bites of his food; then, he begins to break down his day. He went into detail about everything except silent lunch and his unknown stalker. He knew how Shelia Ann was and he didn't want to hear her mouth about getting silent lunch again and he knew she wouldn't let him go down by the pond if she knew he was being followed.

"Well, your day sounded very eventful. There's nothing else you need to tell me?" Shelia Ann asked.

"No Ma'am, nothing I can think of," Jerry said, scratching his head.

"Are you sure?" Jerry begins to fold under the pressure.

"OK, OK, Ma, look, listen, I got silent lunch today but it wasn't my fault."

"Well, whose fault was it?"

"Well, see, what had happened was…"

"Jerry, don't start lying," Shelia Ann said, "choose your next few words wisely."

The one thing she couldn't stand was being lied to. She always told Jerry she would go to war for him, just don't have her looking crazy defending him. Jerry collected his thoughts, looked at his mother and said sorry.

"Sorry for what Jerry? What did you do?"

"I was talking in line while I was waiting on my food, but I wasn't the only one," Jerry said.

"It doesn't matter if you were the only one or not Jerry, you were most definitely one of the ones to suffer the consequences, and that's the bottom line. You're always focusing on the wrong thing once you get in trouble, instead of reflecting on yourself and thinking about what you could have done differently in the situation. You need to think more before you act, because as of now, most of your decisions lately have been careless. So you need to ponder more before you do anything. Your final destination in life is nothing but a sum, an accumulation of choices you've made over your life span." Jerry ate as his mother spoke with him.

"After you finish eating, sweep this floor, get your clothes out for school tomorrow, take a shower, and hurry to bed. No playing around Jerry."

"Yes Ma'am," Jerry said.

He ate, swept the floor, hopped in the shower, and rushed off to bed just like his mother told him to. He already felt as if he was walking on eggshells, so he didn't want to push his luck any further. As he lay in bed, he didn't do his usual pillow talk with his pillows. He thought heavily about what could have been following him down by the pond this evening. He pondered that thought until he fell asleep. He even dreamed about it and in his dream, it was his father following him.

CHAPTER 3

WRONG PLACE, WORSE TIMING

"JERRY!!!" Shelia Ann yells, "wake up and get ready!" Jerry sits straight up out of the bed.

"And where are your clothes? I told you to get them out last night. This is what I am talking about right here Jerry; small things add up to the bigger picture. I gave you clear instructions last night, and you couldn't follow through. Pure laziness."

Jerry honestly had forgotten about that. He had done everything else she asked, but because they were running late again, it was as if Jerry hadn't done anything.

"Get out of that bed, Jerry and hurry up and get ready. Stop looking at me like I'm crazy because if you miss that bus again this morning, I will show you crazy."

Jerry's feet got tangled in the sheets as he stumbled out of the bed. He ran over to his dresser, grabbed a pair of underwear and mixed-matched socks out of the first drawer, a half-wrinkled t-shirt out of the second, and a pair of shorts that stopped right above the knee out of the third. He laid his clothes out on his bed and then went to brush his teeth and wash his face. By the time he got his clothes on, he could hear Shelia Ann yelling at him to get out of the house and down the road to the bus stop before he missed it. He slipped on his blue and white Air Max shoes and grabbed his gold chain with the letter 'J' on it off the top of his dresser.

He rushed out the door shouting, "Love you Ma, have a good day!" Then he took off down the road.

He noticed the other kids were already at the bus stop waiting. About half the distance there he realized he had forgotten his bookbag, but it was too late and he felt like he had already walked too far to turn around now. He could hear the bus approaching, so he started to jog, but when he saw the bus stop and Stacy looked back at him as she was getting on, he picked up the pace. She was a good enough reason for Jerry to aim for perfect attendance. Jerry hopped on the bus breathing heavily and sweating. Stacy was already seated beside one of her girlfriends. Still, her and Jerry made eye contact as he walked the bus aisle. He waved, but she just rolled her eyes and smiled. It was past the middle of the school year at this point, and Jerry was still barely making it to the bus stop on time. Stacy had even given him a few suggestions that she thought might help him, but it was seemingly pointless. She secretly desired for Jerry to get up early enough for them to walk the long dirt path together to the bus stop. She would give him hints and clues of her eagerness.

Stacy would say things like, "It sure does get lonely taking all those steps to the bus stop without anyone to talk to or my backpack is so heavy; I really wish I had someone to help me carry a few books."

Stacy would always say things of that nature, but Jerry for some reason would not catch on. Maybe it was fear blinding his judgment or just out right naiveness.

Usually during the morning bus ride, Jerry would fall into his normal backseat and lean his head up against the window. Then he would tuck his arms inside of his shirt and try to get as much sleep as possible, but between children being loud and the bus driver seeming to hit every pothole the road had to offer, it was hard for Jerry to get some sleep. This particular morning was even harder for Jerry because two girls had gotten into a fight and the other kids responded very dramatically. Kids were jumping up and down in the bus seats, yelling and screaming, throwing objects out the window, etc. It had gotten so bad to the point that the bus driver had to pull over to the side of the road and completely stop the bus in order to diffuse the situation. Jerry was at full attention as the bus driver broke up the two young ladies from fighting. Clothes were ripped, makeup was smeared, and hair was tossed not only between the two young ladies but the bus driver as well. Mrs. Creed, the bus driver, was at her wits end when it came to the students. She was a much older lady who grew up in an era where kids respected authority, and if they didn't, physical punishment was handed out immediately by the closest authority. She made sure the kids knew and understood who she was and where she was from. She didn't play when it came to eating on her bus, jumping from seat to seat, or throwing anything out the window. She was completely furious when it came to the student's behavior and she had plans of writing every single one of them up who had anything to do with the incident on the bus.

By the time Mrs. Creed finally pulled into the school parking lot, she was sweating from head to toe, still infuriated with everyone on the bus. The moment she parked the bus, she slung the double doors open so fast it almost came off the hinges. She told everyone to stay in their seats while she discussed what happened with the assistant principal. Mrs. Creed's story was as dramatic as it could possibly be. By the time she got done telling her story, all the kids were fighting and deserved to be suspended off the bus, as if she were looking for some sort of vacation away from the students.

"They fight, they're loud, and they have no respect for authority," Mrs.

Creed said angrily, "I'm done, I've had enough. I'm sick of these kids and their shenanigans."

Mrs. Creed stormed off to her car, leaving the bus and the students unattended. Needless to say, but that was the last of Mrs. Creed working for the school system. She had reached her breaking point. Now she works part-time at the local supermarket in town. Jerry would see her from time to time when he would go early in the mornings on the weekend to help his mother grocery shop.

As the students exited the bus, each of them could see the rage in the assistant principal's eyes. They knew there would be consequences for their morning actions.

"Jerry! What happened?" the assistant principal asked as soon as he stepped off the bus.

"Now you know I ain't no snitch Miss Davis."

"It's not about being a snitch Jerry; it's about the safety of you and everyone else on the bus, including the driver. She deserves respect and a peace of mind as she transports y'all back and forth from school to home."

Jerry with his eyes wide and his head tilted said, "Dang Miss Davis, you coming for me like I did it."

"Jerry, I just want you to see the bigger picture and the importance of following bus rules. You are popular and very influential amongst the other students. If you pull your weight in the right direction, you would be surprised at how different things would be around here."

Jerry thought about Miss Davis's comments as he walked to breakfast. He had never heard that he was influential or popular. He always thought he was, but it was good to hear it coming from someone else.

On his way to the cafeteria, he passed by the bathrooms, which always smelled bad, but this particular smell was foreign to him. He also heard coughing and dry heaving coming from one of the stalls. A few moments before Jerry approached the bathroom, he saw a few other students stop in front of the bathroom with a very strange look on their faces. He noticed them looking around at each other with disbelief, but none of them would enter; they just paused and kept going past the bathroom. Jerry's curiosity just wouldn't let him keep walking. He had to get to the bottom of whatever that smell was, and he wanted to know who was doing all that coughing. As he entered, he saw a cloud of smoke exiting the bathroom window, coming from the back stall. He quietly tip-toed over to the back stall to see who it was, and once he opened the door, he was greeted with another cloud of smoke blown directly in his face from two very frightened 8th graders at this point. Their hearts dropped down to their stomachs because of how scared they were.

One of the 8th graders pushed Jerry and said, "You play too much man! Get out of here before I make you get out."

Now, Jerry's temper wasn't the best, as we all know, so it didn't take much to get him started. Jerry immediately shoves back, causing a domino effect between the two 8th graders and the object they were smoking. A lot of ruckus was made by the time both 8th graders fell and dropped whatever they were smoking in the toilet. Many people heard the noise coming from the bathroom, including the resource officer, Deputy Duncan. Now, Deputy Duncan was real cool and laid-back. He never gave the students a hard time and they all respected him for the most part. Of course, he had to make an example out of a few students from time to time, but mostly everyone straightened up just off of his presence and stature.

"Boys! What's going on here?" Deputy Duncan said with a deep, stern voice, "and what is that smell? Y'all better not be doing what it smells like y'all doing in here. That's automatic grounds for expulsion." As Deputy Duncan was explaining the consequences of drugs on a drug-free campus, all of a sudden, the toilet flushes.

"That was smart of y'all to get rid of the evidence," said Deputy Duncan, "but let's see how clever y'all are explaining this smell to your principal. Come with me." As they sat and waited anxiously for the principal, Jerry thought about the trouble he would be in once Shelia Ann found out about this.

"Hey man, y'all need to let Principal Stewart know I won't smoking," Jerry said.

"This is all your fault in the first place, Jerry. If you would've minded your own business, we wouldn't be here right now," one of the 8th graders responded.

"Yea, so we definitely saying you were a part of it since you wanted to be so badly," the other 8th grader said.

Jerry looked at both guys with disgust and anger. He actually did not have an issue with either of those guys; it was just under these unforeseen circumstances.

Principal Stewart rushes in abruptly, slamming the door shut behind him and says, "Have y'all lost your minds smoking in my school!" Jerry quickly stands to speak.

"Not a word, Jerry! And I'm tired of your name being brought up every time trouble is presented to me." Jerry hangs his head and flops back down in the seat.

"And you two, what am I going to do with y'all? Every week it's something. Y'all are like Sonic and Tales out here head hunting for trouble." Both young men looked at each other, slightly confused with Principal Stewart's analogy, "now Deputy Duncan shared with me that he only saw a cloud of smoke, but he heard the toilet flush once he made his presence known. Now what am I supposed to assume with that information, fellas? He also mentioned a lot of noise coming from the bathroom, as if you all were fighting." It was so quiet in the office you could hear a mouse pee on cotton.

"Well, somebody say something," Principal Stewart said, "I wasn't talking to the walls behind you."

"Well, all I know is I wasn't smoking," Jerry said with his hands thrown in the air.

"That's not good enough Jerry; that response won't cut it. Have you ever heard of 'guilty by association?'" Principal Stewart asked rhetorically.

"It means you are guilty of committing a crime through just knowing or being attached to someone else, rather than having any hard direct evidence against you."

Jerry leans his head back against the wall and puts his hands over his face. For the moment, all he could think of was Shelia Ann's scripture she would quote to him religiously. He couldn't remember it word for word, but he knew it was **1 Corinthians 15:33** and that it talked about not letting bad company corrupt good character. The only thing is, Jerry wasn't sure if he was the character or the company.

"Still silent, huh? Nobody with any vital information. Well, consider yourselves lucky this time since you weren't caught in the act, but I will still be informing your parents about this situation." To Jerry, that was worse than getting in trouble at school.

"What are you telling if we're not in trouble?" Jerry asked.

"I don't want any of you to feel or think you've gotten away with this. You all need to understand the severity of having drugs on campus."

"But I wasn't even smoking."

"You're missing the point Jerry; my decision is final."

Sitting in class, it was hard for Jerry to concentrate. The only thing on his mind was the lashing or worse, she might confiscate his speaker and fishing rods. Jerry lived for fishing and hearing new sounds. At that time, Jerry would've done anything to rewind time. If he could go back to last night when he was preparing for bed, he would. It just wasn't a good jump start to the day, considering that first period wasn't even halfway through yet. His body language was horrible and he was completely disengaged from the lesson being taught. English class is Jerry's 1st block of the day. He was never too fond of reading and writing, and on top of that, his mind was in a different space than his body. He couldn't get out of his own head. During class, the instructor handed out a list of words that needed to be defined. It was a list of about 20 different words, but it seemed as if Jerry was running into words that were describing his morning. Words like disappointment, failure, dismay, curiosity, and so on and so forth were sticking out to him like a sore thumb. It only made him more and more upset defining each of those words.

"Jerry are you OK?" the English instructor asked with concern. Jerry wouldn't respond.

"Jerry, do you hear me talking to you."

"Yes, I hear you. Can you leave me alone now," Jerry replied.

"Now, whatever your issue is, I'm not the reason for it, Jerry. Your negativity is not needed, nor is it called for. I will gladly leave you alone but you don't have to be rude." Jerry just puts his head down on the desk.

"No Sir, now I said I wouldn't bother you, but that doesn't mean you're not going to get your work done. Sit up in that seat and define those words, young man."

Jerry slung the worksheet, the piece of paper, and the pencil onto the floor. Almost making contact with the English instructor as he stood up, he said, "Now, for someone who teaches English, why is it so hard for you to understand it? LEAVE ME ALONE!!!"

Jerry storms out without permission, slamming the door shut and heading straight for the bathroom. As he was walking the hall, Mr. Henry, the school counselor, was exiting the staff bathroom.

"Jerry what's wrong?" Jerry just kept walking.

"I always respect you enough to acknowledge you when you call for me Jerry and I expect the same in return."

Jerry had a certain respect for Mr. Henry; he reminded him of his dad in so many ways, that's why he looked up to him as much as he did. So after Mr. Henry's statement, Jerry turned around, walked up to him, and just vented. He released all of his frustration from this morning unto Mr. Henry's ear gates. After an earful of discrepancies, Mr. Henry calmed Jerry's mindset with a few words of wisdom.

He said, "Jerry, if you had $100 in your hand right now, and you lost $10 or $10 was stolen from you, would you hold tighter to that $90 you have left over or would you give up on the remaining $90?" Jerry thought deeply about what was said.

"No need for a response, just food for thought," Mr. Henry said as he patted Jerry on the back, "now get on back to class, you have a lot more to offer this day, go make the best of it."

Mr. Henry uplifted Jerry's spirit, with his $100 analogy he used. Jerry liked money, and it seemed to have made so much sense, the way Mr. Henry broke it down to him. Unfortunately, by the time Jerry reentered into the classroom, his punishment had already been decided. He had made things worse for himself because of his previous actions. He had been written up for disrupting and skipping class. Those actions would place him in I.S.S. for the remainder of the day.

"Collect your things and report to the I.S.S. Room immediately."

"But…"

"No butts Jerry, I've tried being patient and remaining positive with you, but you literally slammed the door in my face. I'm done with it and I'm done with you for today Jerry. Grab your things and go!"

Considering Jerry forgot his backpack, there wasn't much to collect other than the list of words, scratch paper, and pencil he threw off of the desk. Angrily he grabbed his items and headed for the I.S.S. Room. On his way, he glanced at a piece of paper taped to the wall that read baseball tryouts coming soon and you must have a physical form filled out and completed before attending. Jerry had never played baseball for a team before, and his only experience was down by the pond, where he would at times toss a rock in the air and hit it as hard as he could across the water. He had pretty good hand eye coordination. The only thing was, the sheet

Jerry was reading was a week old and today was the second day of tryouts. So he had already missed one day of tryouts, and he would have no choice but to miss today's session because he wasn't equipped with cleats nor a glove.

On top of that, once you are assigned to I.S.S., you are not to participate in any after-school function on that day. You either wait for your bus to be called or go stand in the car rider line. The odds were already stacked against him. There was only one more day of tryouts left and Jerry wanted to be a part of it, so once he entered the I.S.S. Room he was on his best behavior so that one day of consequences would not turn into two.

CHAPTER 4

IN SCHOOL SUSPENSION

Jerry did not know what was in store for him today in I.S.S., but he would have a rude awakening. The moment he took a step into the room, Mr. Howell, the I.S.S. teacher, stopped him in his tracks.

"Don't take another step young man. Tell me your name, what teacher sent you and why you were assigned to my classroom."

There were about four others already in I.S.S. by the time Jerry showed up, and they all were looking up at Jerry, waiting for his response. For a second, Jerry froze with a blank look on his face.

"Speak young man, didn't you hear what I asked you?" Jerry struggles but finally forms his mouth to respond to Mr. Howell's question.

"My, my name is Jerry and Mrs. Jenkins, the English teacher, sent me to you because I was skipping and disrupting the class. Well…so she says anyway."

"Well, you tell me from your perception what happened Jerry."

"Well, from my view, she kept on antagonizing me after I asked her to leave me alone, but she wouldn't. So I got angry and lashed out at her, but I bet she didn't tell you she kept picking at me."

"Now Jerry," Mr. Howell said sternly, "was she picking on you or holding you accountable for your actions?" Jerry was speechless for the moment, "Exactly, there is a big difference, have a seat and get started on your work."

As Jerry sat quietly and worked, it did not take much for him to be distracted. Jerry was very much in tune with his surroundings. He noticed one of the students had their phone in between the book they were supposed to be reading, another kept on shaking his leg and tapping his pencil, and another just stared at Jerry, watching his every move. Of course, Jerry didn't like that, and he was a few seconds away from letting that particular student know he didn't like it, but the only thing that stopped him was the thought of baseball tryouts. He knew he had to tread lightly. He didn't want to make things worse. It was still early in the morning, and Jerry didn't want any parts of I.S.S. again tomorrow. Especially with the agenda at hand today in I.S.S., there was no way he could go through this again. He and the other four students in the room had to complete their class assignments by lunchtime because, after their silent lunch, it was time to go to work.

During this time of the year, it's basketball season, so the gym, as usual, is trashed with Gatorade bottles, candy wrappers, soda cans, Nacho trays, and much more. So right after lunch, they headed over to the gymnasium, already equipped with gloves, trash cans, and a couple of brooms. One student was instructed to sweep all up and down the gym floor, and the other four were split up. Two on each side of the court, cleaning under the bleachers. Jerry's luck ended him up on the side with the guy staring at him in the I.S.S. Room, which made him feel uncomfortable, and when Jerry felt uncomfortable, he usually resorted to fighting.

First, they had to pull the bleachers out, but it must be simultaneous, in perfect harmony. If not, one side of the bleachers would jam and it would be hard to get them all the way pulled out.

"Come on, man," Jerry said, "pull your side of the bleachers out; you got me doing most of the work over here."

Anthony, which was the name of the young man Jerry was speaking to, still never said a word, he just continued staring at Jerry, but he did at least pull his side of the bleachers. As they began to clean up under the bleachers, all of a sudden, a Gatorade bottle came flying past Jerry's head. As soon as he looks in the direction from which the bottle came, there comes another that hits him right between the eyes. That was all Jerry's temper needed. All you could hear under the bleachers was rumbling and tumbling. Mr. Howell came running under the bleachers, bent at a 90-degree angle to stop the two young men from fighting. Deputy Duncan bent at the same angle and came running from the other side of the bleachers to break up the fight as well. Mr. Howell had Jerry by the arm and Deputy Duncan had Anthony. Once they all came from under the bleachers, the damage was very noticeable on both of the boys. Not only were their clothes torn and stretched out, but Jerry had a knot on his forehead from the Gatorade bottle and Anthony had a black eye from Jerry getting one good punch in before they were pulled away from each other.

"What's the meaning of all this?"

Deputy Duncan asked Anthony, "Why were y'all fighting?"

Anthony was calm, but he still wouldn't say a word. Jerry was still very much excited about the incident, so it made it hard to comprehend what he was saying. Deputy Duncan escorted both of them to the office. As they sat there waiting on Principal Stewart, Jerry began to think about how life was over for him as he knew it.

"My mom is going to kill me," he said under his breath, "and I'm going to miss out on baseball tryouts."

He looks over at Anthony, ready to attack because he feels like Anthony is the reason he was sitting in the principal's office again in the first place.

"I can't even get my work done because of students fighting and being mischievous all over this school. You would think you all would behave yourselves, considering the next step after this is O.S.S."

"Now, why were y'all fighting?" Jerry immediately tells his side of the story.

"Well, Principal Stewart, I was minding my own business cleaning under the bleachers, and he just started throwing Gatorade bottles at me. One of them hit me right between the eyes and it really hurt, so I just blanked out and next thing you know Mr. Howell was pulling me off of him."

"Is that how it happened Anthony? Let me hear your side of the story."

"Right! Please, let's hear your side!" Jerry said passionately.

"No need for an echo Jerry; I'm sure he heard me just fine." Anthony drops his head but still doesn't say a word.

"This would be a great time for you to speak up for yourself young man." Anthony looks up with his eyes full of water while sniffing and wiping his nose with his arm sleeve.

"Umm, well I just…, uh."

"You just what Son?" Principal Stewart said impatiently, as if Anthony were his own child.

"I don't know, I can't remember."

"You can't remember?" Principal Stewart said with his eyes wide, "well, I would advise you to remember something because, as of now, it looks as if you're at fault." Anthony finally spills his guts.

"Yea, I did it, and I'll do it again to anyone trying to steal my girlfriend from me." Both Principal Stewart and Jerry glanced at each other with shock with both ears pinned back and eyes glued on Anthony, ready for the finale of this story, he continued on.

"Jerry knows I like Stacy, yet he is always smiling in her face, passing her notes, and finding some way to get her attention."

"That's what this is about Bro, a girl!" Jerry says as his head tilts to the side.

"Quiet Jerry, let him finish. You had your time to talk without interruption, so give him the same respect." Jerry turns and looks out the office window at the maintenance crew cutting grass in order to keep from talking.

"I've been liking her since the 5th grade and everyone knows it," Anthony said, "and now all of a sudden, this year, Jerry likes her, and everybody saying they would make such a cute couple." Jerry began to chuckle a little, but he played it off as coughing once Principal Stewart and Anthony looked his way.

"Jerry, step outside of my office and go wait at the front with Miss Stevens until I call for you."

"Yes Sir," Jerry said as he hopped up and exited the room.

"Now Anthony, I understand you're hurting, but that doesn't excuse any of your actions today. You assaulted another young man because you let your feelings get the best of you and that is unacceptable. Not only will there be consequences for your actions, but you also owe Jerry an apology." Anthony smacks his lips, folds his arms, and leans back in the chair angrily as if his story was justifiable for his reasoning.

"Fix your demeanor, young man. Sit up when I'm talking to you and look me in the eyes."

"Stand on what you did and take responsibility for it."

Anthony sits up with his shoulders hunched and hands out, looking at Principal Stewart in the eyes and says, "Yea, but Jerry got what he deserved."

"No Anthony," Principal Stewart said, "more like you got what you deserved." Anthony looked with confusion.

"Young man, do you know anything about Isaac Newton and his laws of thermodynamics?" Anthony looked as if Principal Stewart were speaking Pig Latin, "his 3rd law states that for every action, there is an equal and opposite reaction. In other words, what you did to Jerry under the bleachers today was deserving of the same energy reciprocated back to you." Anthony thought about what was just said to him as he dropped his head.

"Don't hang your head Anthony; this isn't a loss, it's a lesson. And another thing, I heard you say that you liked Stacy, but that doesn't make her your girlfriend. Does she like you? Better yet, have you shared with her your feelings towards her?"

Anthony looks up and says, "No I haven't."

"Well how can you be mad at anyone, when you are making the choice to not express yourself. Time waits for no one or nothing, so seize every moment and opportunity that you can. Don't ever look back and have regrets on something you wish you could've done, all because you didn't take advantage of an opportunity once it presented itself. Have some courage about yourself. Understand that fear does nothing but hold you back and that rejection only makes you stronger," Anthony began to smile as those words of wisdom passed through his ear gates, "with all that being said Anthony, you still have to answer to what you did today. So I'm assigning you three days of O.S.S, which is plenty of time for you to think and ponder on some of the things we have discussed today."

"But what about Jerry?" Anthony asked.

"Don't worry about Jerry, only yourself and your actions. Now go out into the front with Miss Stevens and wait for your ride, I will be giving your parents a call informing them of what happened and that you will need to be picked up immediately." Anthony stands, drags his feet towards the door, and exits quietly.

Principal Stewart calls the front desk and says, "Miss Stevens, can you send Jerry back into my office please and thank you."

"Yes Sir, no problem, he's on his way now."

As Jerry enters the room, Principal Stewart says, "What am I going to do with you Jerry? This is the second time today you've been in my office."

"I was defending myself in both situations today Principal Stewart."

"Yea, but also, in both situations, you had the chance to walk away. The thing about self-defense is that it really only applies when someone is continuously attacking you, and you have to do whatever you have to do in order to stop the attack. Don't get me wrong, I know a lot of you were raised in this school to choose violence first if someone hits you, but you and all your parents still have to understand that there will still be consequences for those actions. Choosing not to tell a teacher first and deciding to take matters into your own hands is considered being a vigilante out in the real world, and you will still be arrested for actions, even though you feel like it's the right thing to do." Jerry understood where Principal Stewart was coming from, but he had always believed that as long as he didn't swing first, he would be in the clear of any trouble.

"So Jerry, with all of that being said, I am assigning you one day of

O.S.S. That will give you one day to think about your actions. You will be allowed to come back to school on Friday."

"Friday!" Jerry said loudly, "but the last day of baseball tryouts is tomorrow."

"That's true Jerry, tomorrow is the last day of baseball tryouts. Did you have knowledge of that before or after your incident with Anthony?"

"Before," Jerry said while putting his hand over his face.

"Make eye contact when speaking or being spoken to, no matter what the situation is. Stand on your failures as strongly as your accomplishments. One is your left, and the other your right. So in other words, you can't have one without the other in order to reach your destination. Learn from your failures and stay humble but strategic through every accomplishment. You must find ways to build upon your success while minimizing your shortcomings."

Jerry sat quietly as Principal Stewart continued to lecture him. He was listening, but his thought process wasn't all the way there. He began to think about the type of punishment Sheila Ann would deliver. Jerry wasn't quite sure how being suspended from school worked out for other kids in their homes, but for Jerry, he knew that meant double the amount of chores, no fishing, no speaker, and sometimes a lashing across the behind, depending on what he had said or done. Plus, he could not stop thinking about the fact of missing the last day of baseball tryouts tomorrow. He started to feel overwhelmed thinking of the hole he had dug himself into, so his eyes began to water and the palms of his hands became very clammy.

"Jerry! Are you listening to me?" Principal Stewart asked.

"Yes Sir," Jerry said.

"Well, answer my question, are you a bus or car rider?"

"Bus rider," Jerry said as he wiped his eyes.

"OK well, head back down to the I.S.S. Room and wait on your bus to be called."

Jerry stands and drags slowly out of the room with his head down as he walks back into the I.S.S. Room quietly. Anthony, on the other hand, was told to remain at the front desk as he awaited his ride.

CHAPTER 5

OUT OF SCHOOL

Before Jerry left from Principal Stewart's office, he was given a piece of paper with his one-day suspension and a detailed description of why he was being suspended. As he sat in I.S.S. for the remainder of the day, he kept looking over his suspension papers, shaking his head in disbelief. Before he knew it, Miss Stevens was speaking over the intercom, releasing car and bus riders. Any other day, on the bus ride home, it seemed like it took forever for the bus driver to pull up to his particular bus stop, but not today. Today seemed as if the driver skipped all the stops in front of Jerry's and decided to get him off first. Not only that, but Jerry was also uninterested in beatboxing or any type of freestyle session in the back of the bus like usual. He just sat quietly and thought about how Shelia Ann was going to react the moment he walked through the door.

"I know my momma gone trip," Jerry says to himself as the bus comes to a stop in front of the long dirt path.

Honestly, for some reason, the dirt path wasn't so long. Seemed like the shorter his steps, the closer the trees at the end of the path got. Stacy noticed the worry in Jerry's face as they walked home and she tried her best to comfort him.

"It's going to be OK Jerry," Stacy says as her fingers lock with his.

"So, what's up with you and Ant?" Jerry asked sorta aggressively as he pulled his hand away from hers.

"What?" Stacy said shockingly, "what are you talking about and where did that come from?" Jerry acted as if he didn't hear her and kept right on walking home.

"Oh, so you're ignoring me now Jerry?" Stacy asked as she stopped in her tracks. Jerry looks back but continues to walk.

"You can be so mean at times Jerry," Stacy says as she stomps her way towards him, "you sound so jealous when all you had to do was ask."

"I did ask and I couldn't have been any clearer than I was with my question," Jerry said sarcastically.

"Yea, but you were rude about it and that is unnecessary," Stacy replied as she rolled her eyes and neck.

"Do you plan on answering the question or not?" Jerry asked.

"Do you plan on listening, or do you already have an answer made up in your head?" Jerry smacks his lips.

By this time, they had both reached the end of the dirt road.

"We will discuss this more tomorrow when I get home from school, Jerry. Do you think you could meet me down by the pond tomorrow once I get off the bus?"

Jerry thought for a minute, but not about the question she asked. It was more like, what did she know about being down by the pond? Jerry went almost every day but he never saw Stacy down there. His mind began to wonder if she was the one watching and following him last night when he ran home.

"Down by the pond, you say? What do you know of the pond? I fish down there almost every day and I have never seen you."

"I walk down there from time to time just to clear my head and I also enjoy talking to Mother Nature. She listens well and she holds all my secrets dear to her heart."

"Yea, whatever," Jerry said, "I doubt my momma gone let me out the house anyway." Jerry turned and looked towards his house. Shelia Ann was standing at the screen door with nothing but fire in her eyes.

"Boy, get in this house! If it wasn't for my gas already being low in my tank, I would've come down to that schoolhouse and showed you how to act a fool right in front of your friends since that's what you doing anyway, I was gone really put on a show for you. You did everything in that school but learn today, oh but you gone learn this good day, now hurry up and get in my house."

Jerry didn't even say bye to Stacy. He was too embarrassed to turn around and everything Stacy said about it being OK went right out the window the moment she heard Jerry's mom going off on him. Stacy felt so bad for Jerry, but there was nothing she could do about it. So she ran off into her house at full speed so no one could see her feeling sorry for Jerry. As Jerry was walking up the steps of his house, he noticed the belt wrapped around Shelia Ann's hand, swinging low down by her ankles.

"Come on in here boy, you run in this house any other day. Don't let this belt slow you down."

"Momma, please, today was a big misunderstanding. You gotta believe me."

"Junior, the only thing I believe is that you're lying to me right now. Point blank, period. Now get in this house!" Shelia Ann yells to the top of her lungs.

Jerry's heart dropped down into his stomach. He was so scared he felt sick. He quickly dodges into the house, trying his best to escape the lashing, but Shelia Ann's aim is magnificent. She could crack that belt across Jerry's behind better than any plantation owner cracking their whip across the back of a slave. She was so good at it that, at times, Jerry wondered what side of history she would have been on during those times.

"Momma, I'm so sorry," Jerry cries out as he runs around the house, ducking and dodging the belt in his mother's hand.

"Be still Jerry, you're only making it worse for yourself."

Jerry continued to move. He ran around the kitchen counter, slid under the bed, ducked behind the couch, etc., but Shelia Ann was right behind him at every turn. She might have been a little overweight, but she could move and move well. By the time she got done whooping Jerry, the house was a mess. She was tired and Jerry was sobbing on the living room floor.

"Hush up Junior, before I get you again," Shelia Ann says as she tries to catch her breath, "I told you to be still. I ought to get you again anyway for not listening. Now go cut on the ceiling fan and get this house back straight. You have exactly one hour to get this house back right, take a shower, and sit down at my table ready to eat. There will be no extracurricular activity for you tonight or all day tomorrow. After you eat, head straight to bed, and I mean it, Junior, straight to bed. There will be a list of chores you will need to have done by the time I get home from work, and I expect every one of them to be done efficiently and adequately. I don't want to hear any excuses, I just want to see it done when I arrive or else..."

Jerry looks up with complete fear in his eyes and says, "Or else what Ma?"

"Boy don't ever question nor play with me. You know exactly what I mean by 'or else' now go do what I said before 'or else' starts happening right now. Jerry hops up quickly to go and turn on the ceiling fan.

"Whew! Thank you, Jesus," Shelia Ann says to herself as the fan starts to circulate air all around the room.

The air was also a sense of relief to Jerry as well, considering the sweat falling from his forehead and the heat rising from his hind part. As he was cleaning the mess he and Shelia Ann made, she began speaking with him about choices.

"Junior as you get older, you will realize that everything is not clear cut, black and white. What I mean by that is it's not all about right or wrong but more about the decisions you make. Every choice you make will affect your life positively or negatively, but that will be up to you. For instance, if you brush your teeth, your mouth will smell refreshing. If not, your breath will smell disgusting. Everything boils down to a choice, especially when it comes to your time. You have to learn to <u>invest</u>, not spend your time. Be productive with your time because time looks back for no one. There is nothing in this world you can do to get back the day you wasted by sitting in the office and I.S.S. all day."

Jerry cleaned while he listened to Shelia Ann drop knowledge on him. Some things he understood, and some he didn't, but he wouldn't dare ask any questions. He would just nod his head as he continued cleaning.

"Jerry, remember you only have an hour to get done cleaning and in the shower. So tighten up, so you can eat and go to bed. I promise your day tomorrow will be productive. The list of chores and duties will be posted on the refrigerator and…."

All of a sudden, the phone rings, but Shelia Ann can't really recognize the number. She almost waits for it to go to voicemail but finally decides to answer.

"Hello, Hello!" She says again, already getting impatient.

Once, a familiar voice responded with, "Hello, Shelia Ann, it's been a long time." Her eyes widened.

She hopped up, glanced over at Jerry, and told him to go ahead and take a shower. She quickly moved to her room and shut the door. Jerry thought it was weird how she just stopped talking and wanted him to stop cleaning and go shower. His curiosity just wouldn't let him follow simple instructions. He had to know why his mother's whole demeanor changed after she answered the phone. Jerry tiptoed lightly as he placed his head and ear up against the door as softly as he could in order to hear without being heard.

"You said you loved me, you said you loved us," Jerry heard his mom say, "and you made so many broken promises that till this day I am still piecing back together. You broke my heart and you broke this family. Never again will you see your son and I will make sure of that. I don't want any of your selfish ways rubbing off on him. Now get off my phone and don't you ever call back, you worthless excuse of a man."

Shelia Ann hangs up abruptly and breaks down. Jerry sat on the floor outside of his mom's door and listened to her weep. He didn't quite understand exactly what was going on, but he had an idea. All he knew at the moment, for sure, was that Shelia Ann was hurting, and he couldn't stand hearing or seeing her cry. It caused his heart to ache, and it made him angry to the point of water filling his eyes because he felt like there was nothing he could do to fix the situation. Jerry knocked on the door lightly.

"Ma, are you OK?"

"Go take a shower like I said Junior!" Shelia Ann shouts. Jerry rushes off to the bathroom to prepare for his shower.

Once he was done showering, Shelia Ann had his plate hot and ready sitting on the kitchen table. She had made meatloaf with mac-n-cheese and green beans, one of Jerry's favorite dishes.

"OOOOO…Ma, you done it again, you be going loco in the kitchen."

Shelia Ann doesn't say a word. It's crazy how loud her silence was. Jerry was scared to ask again, but he couldn't help it. He loved his mother so much and it burdened him to see her like this.

"Ma, are you OK?" Jerry asked with knots in his stomach.

"And what makes you think something is wrong Junior? Were you and all your nosiness listening in on my conversation?"

"No, No, No, Ma, I'm only asking because the food tastes extra good tonight and I know you really throw down in the kitchen when you are upset about something?"

"Umhumm! Let me find out you're going around here making me mad on purpose in order for the food to taste better."

Jerry chuckles a little and says, "No Ma, I never want to make you angry intentionally. I love to see you smile." Next, Jerry asked about her phone call as if he wasn't listening.

"What conversation are you talking about, though Ma?"

"Don't play with me Junior, I know you were ear hustling."

"No Ma, I wasn't ear hustling, I just heard you crying, that's all."

"But how did you hear me crying when you were supposed to be on the other side of the house getting ready to take a shower."

For the moment, Jerry was speechless. Shelia Ann was waiting for a response, staring at him with a slight grin on her face because she thought it was cute how concerned Jerry was with her feelings. She also felt like Jerry knew it was his father on the other line because of how loud she was speaking and what she was speaking about. Jerry had a good feeling about who she may have been yelling at on the phone, but he wasn't 100%, which is why he kept on asking questions. The more questions he would ask, the more Shelia Ann would deflect. She seemed to never answer questions straightforward when it came to Jerry Sr., but that still wouldn't keep Junior from asking.

"Stop talking and finish eating your food Junior. Really, by now, you are already supposed to be in bed. No more questions for tonight."

Jerry finished his food, stood up from the table and said, "Wow, that was good, Ma. You must've been furious while you were cooking tonight."

"That mouth of yours is going to get you in more trouble than you are already in Junior. Stop trying to be funny all the time. Just saying that the food was good would have been sufficient enough. I don't need any extra comments."

"Yes Ma'am," Jerry said.

"Now put your plate, cup, and silverware in the sink with the rest of the dirty dishes. The dishes and a lot of other chores will be waiting for you first thing in the morning. So you need to make sure you get some good rest tonight because you will work and work only tomorrow. There will be no TV, no cellphone, no tablet, no laptop, no speaker, and you better not leave this house, so no fishing. I am so sick of you getting into fights and getting into mischievous acts. From now on, I promise you will regret getting suspended. Goodnight Junior!"

As Jerry tossed and turned in bed, he wondered what his mother meant by regretting this suspension. He couldn't sleep for a while because his mind wouldn't rest. Eventually, he dozed off and before he knew it, his mother was standing over him the next morning.

"Junior, wake up," Shelia Ann says in a stern voice. As Jerry was opening his eyes, she began to debrief him on his day before she left for work.

"Junior, I have made you breakfast and it is sitting in the microwave. For lunch, just eat some snacks, maybe a hot pocket or some cereal. Choose one or the other Junior, don't eat a hole in my kitchen and I mean it."

Jerry could barely keep his eyes open. He had never blinked so much before in his life. He wondered how early it was and why she couldn't just text him all the information she felt the need to run down in detail at this very moment.

"Junior!" She yelled as she sees his eyes begin to fade again, "sit up and listen."

Jerry sits up, sighs, wipes his eyes, and says, "Yes Ma'am."

"Your itinerary for the day is posted on the refrigerator, like I told you last night. After you finish something on the list, I need you to put a checkmark beside it so that I will know you got it done. I will also be walking around this house once I get home from work, making sure you got everything done that you checked off. Another thing, I expect you to finish everything I put on that list. No exceptions Junior, get it done."

She kissed him on the forehead, told him how much she loved him and then exited the room. Jerry sat up long enough to hear the car crank, the car door close, and the wheels spinning away from their single-wide trailer. He immediately buried himself under the covers and went back to sleep. He thought to himself *that he might as well be fully rested before starting his day, instead of going ahead and getting started early.*

It comes down to small everyday choices like Jerry is facing right now, that stunts people's growth, their blessing, and their opportunity to be great. So many people, like Jerry, choose sleep, procrastination, or any other short-term satisfaction instead of long-term gratification.

CHAPTER 6

CONQUERING THE LIST

Well, as time was doing as it always does Jerry again was taking her seconds for granted. He didn't realize that he had slept over half the day away. It was going on past 1:30 p.m., and he still had an entire list of chores that needed to be completed. Shelia Ann got off work at 3:00 p.m., and it took her about 20 to 30 minutes to get home, give or take heavy traffic or her having to run a few errands before coming in. This gave Jerry approximately two hours to have every task completed on the list. Task one involved reading and writing about a chapter novel Shelia Ann had sitting on the kitchen table. He thought he would outsmart Shelia Ann by looking up the story on Google, but he soon realized she wasn't playing about no electronics. She had taken his phone, his speaker, she had unplugged the television and taken the cord, and there wasn't a tablet or laptop in sight.

"Wow! Momma got real dramatic with this one," Jerry says as he continues to look for any type of electronic device.

While he is looking, suddenly he hears a car door slam and his heart immediately drops down into his stomach. Jerry was terrified. He ran to the couch, fingers shaking, causing the blind shades to vibrate as he peeked through, only to realize it was Stacy and her dad. Jerry blew a sigh of relief. He really thought Shelia Ann had come home early. Quickly, his thought process shifted to Stacy as he saw her dad open her car door and help her out of the passenger seat. He noticed she was hunched over, holding her stomach. He wondered what could possibly be wrong and is she was okay. He wanted to burst outside, run right over to her and ask, but the sight of her dad always put a sense of fear in Jerry. So he decided to just keep peeking through the blinds. As she was entering the house, Jerry figured she would go straight to her room, so he ran to his room and waited by the window, hoping she would pass by soon. As he waited, he thought about that list of chores Shelia Ann had posted on the refrigerator.

"Man! It's going on 2 o'clock and I haven't even started yet. Hurry up, Stacy, what you got going on."

Jerry decides he can't wait any longer. He stands up, takes about one step away from his seat, and then here comes Stacy passing by her window. He quickly sits back down. She never did come back to the window, but Jerry did notice her dad hop back in his truck and leave swiftly. Just watching her dad do that upset him a little bit. His mind immediately flashed back to when he was standing in the screen door with an ice-cold alcoholic beverage, watching his dad drive out of his life. By the time he sped off, Stacy was coming out of the front door and looking directly into Jerry's window. Jerry's heart began to drop again but he played it off cool. He nodded his head in an upward motion and smiled. That was his way of saying what's up. She had a slight smirk on her face, with her hands on her hips.

"Come here Jerry," she says as she rolls her eyes. Jerry runs to the door but walks outside smoothly over to Stacy.

"What's up Stacy," Jerry says as he looks away from her.

"Oh, so that's what we doing now? We not making eye contact when we talk. OK, I see how it is. Are you still mad at me from yesterday over something I didn't even do?" Jerry switches the topic, which only makes Stacy even more upset.

"Look, my mama left this chapter book that she wants me to write about," Jerry tells her the title and then asks if she knows anything about the book. There was a pure fire in Stacy's eyes. She was so furious.

"So you're going to act like I didn't just ask you a question?" Jerry switches the topic again.

"I saw your dad helping you out of the car once y'all pulled up, but you were hunched over, holding your stomach, as if something were wrong. You look perfectly fine now, so what was that all about?" Stacy gets quiet for a moment and then tries to change the subject herself.

"Oh no," Jerry says, "you're not gonna wiggle your way out of this one. What was all that about?"

"Don't worry about it, just girl stuff," Stacy says.

"Wow, that's crazy so that you can blow off a question, but I can't. Oh OK, I get it now."

"It's not even like that Jerry. Do you wanna know that badly?"

"Yes, as a matter of fact, I do."

"Fine, since you asked for it. There is a certain time of the month, every month when my body feels as if it's going through some weird changes inside and out. I become very emotional and sometimes a bit frightened. It's just me and my dad here, so when it happened for the first time about three or four months ago, I was terrified and so was he, even though he acted as if he wasn't. I didn't know what was going on exactly. I just knew it felt like someone was twisting my guts in a counterclockwise motion and blood was running down my legs." Jerry with eyes and mouth wide open, was speechless as she continued.

"So my dad came down to sign me out of school today, because I was starting to have that weird, painful feeling in my stomach, and he already knows how bad it gets for me. He knows that the first two or three days of my cycle are the worst, so he takes extra good care of me. No matter what I want, he would it get for me," Stacy says, smiling.

"Your cycle?" Jerry repeated confusingly.

"Yes Jerry, it is called a menstrual cycle or period. Most girls have it every month once they reach a certain age. It may vary, depending on the girl and how her body reacts. Some are regularly every month and others are irregular, so their body may skip a month or so, but it's still something that girls have to go through no matter what."

"Oh, so it's nothing boys have to ever worry about?" Stacy rolls her eyes and chuckles.

"No Jerry, it's not anything boys have to worry about." Jerry looks to the sky and blows a sigh of relief.

"Wow, you really had me scared for a second there. Sure is good to be a boy," Jerry says with such a selfish grin on his face.

"Whatever Jerry, I'm pretty sure you saw my dad speed off too, huh?"

"Yea, I did, he seemed to be in a big rush," Jerry responded.

"Well, he was he has to get back to work."

"Oh OK, where does your pops work?"

"Down at the factory."

"Does he like to fish?"

"Naw, not really."

"Well, what about sports?"

"No, he's not really into sports either. He reads a lot and loves to work out, but why are you asking so many questions about my dad?"

"Just curious," Jerry says, "my pops walked out on me and my mom a few years back and since the day he left, I always wonder how things would be if he stuck around. I wonder if I have any other brothers or sisters out there. If so, do they know about me? I wonder about the tone of his voice when he says my name. Is he proud or disappointed about what he helped create? And the main thing, like the two biggest things. Why did you leave and do you even love me?"

Stacy with water in her eyes says, "Wow, Jerry, It really sounds like you're hurting. I can't relate exactly to your story, but I can feel your pain. The pain of missing someone and wondering what it would be like to just spend a day with them." Jerry looks at her with a puzzled look on his face.

"What are you talking about Stacy?" She wipes her eyes and begins to tell Jerry the story of her mom.

"Well Jerry," as she sniffles, "I never met my mom. She died giving birth to me; I have so many questions and so many thoughts that haven't been confronted or dealt with. I blame myself every day for her not being here, and I think my dad blames me at times as well. He has never come out and said anything. It's just the way he looks at me sometimes. To be honest, it's actually the way he doesn't look at me. My own father won't make eye contact with me for more than 15 seconds at a time. I've seen some pictures of my mom, and I do resemble her a lot. I think that may also be the reason he won't really look at me. I'm not exactly sure, but I know I'm missing my mom on a physical level and my dad emotionally." Jerry, again, was speechless after Stacy's words.

"Dang Stacy, I'm so sorry to hear that. I never knew, I mean, I did always wonder, but I just assumed your parents split."

"I wish that was the case," Stacy replied, "at least then that would give me a chance to see her."

"Well, you know they always say the apple doesn't fall too far away from the tree. So with that being said, she must've been a cool lady because you sure are."

"Aww, thanks Jerry, that was sweet and your dad just doesn't know what he is missing out on. You're the coolest, funniest, and most fearless person I know." Jerry blushed with his head down and smiled a little.

"Thank you Stacy. That would mean so much coming from my dad. I just wanna hear him say things like that and show me new things."

Jerry was so wrapped up in his conversation with Stacy he completely forgot about the list of chores on the refrigerator. At this point, time had pushed past 2:30 p.m.

"Oh snap," Jerry said shockingly, "I gotta go."

"Why the rush?" Stacy asked.

"My mother left me like a whole list of chores to do on the refrigerator, and I only have about one hour left to get everything done. Aww man, she's gonna kill me, bring me back to life, then kill me again." Stacy giggles as Jerry breaks down.

"I'll help you Jerry. What's on the agenda?"

"Help me! How are you going to help me? My mother would peel the skin off my backside if she ever knew I had a girl in the house without her knowing about it."

"Well, good thing our windows are facing each other so that whenever your mom steps through the front door, I'll climb out of your room window."

For a second, Jerry was confused. He felt like the roles were being reversed because of the way Stacy was talking. Her idea made him feel like he was the goodie goodie boy and that she was bad, but with a very convincing argument. Jerry liked the idea, and he loved that Stacy came up with it.

He grabbed her by the hand, pulling her in the direction of his house saying, "Sounds like a plan to me. It's a lot that has to get done, so we gotta hurry up."

As they rush into the house, Stacy reminds Jerry of the conversation they were supposed to be finishing from yesterday. Jerry looks off and rolls his eyes.

"Don't do that, Jerry, you really hurt my feelings yesterday, so don't dismiss them like they don't matter."

"You're right Stacy, so before we get started, let me apologize for coming at you sideways yesterday. I was having a bad day but I never should have taken it out on you. Please forgive me."

"You right, you shouldn't have taken it out on me, but I forgive you. It's water under the bridge now. So, let's tackle this list." Jerry runs and snatches it off the refrigerator.

Other than the first task which involved reading and writing, everything else was a cleaning type of task. Task number two stated to vacuum and or sweep every room in the house except her room. Shelia Ann's room was always off limits. Especially if she wasn't there, somehow she could tell anything moved out from its original spot. She kept her bed spread creased, so that she would be able to notice if anyone was on her bed for whatever reason.

"OK Jerry, I'll start on task two for you. Where is your broom and vacuum cleaner?" As he was grabbing the cleaning equipment for Stacy, she continued to read the list of chores out loud.

"Task three! Take out all trash in the house and replace the bins with new trash bags."

Jerry hands her the vacuum cleaner and then leans the broom up against the front door where she can see it and says, "Don't worry, I got that. What's the next task."

"No Jerry, we are not about to skip all over this list. Go ahead and take all the trash out first. Make sure you hurry up because we still have to sit down and work on that first task when we get done with everything else."

By the time Jerry was finished taking out the trash, Stacy was already about done sweeping and vacuuming, plus she was running hot soapy water in the kitchen sink to prepare washing dishes.

"Dang, you move fast," Jerry said in shock.

"No Jerry," Stacy said, giggling, "you're just slow."

"Go ahead and start on the fifth task because I am about to start on the fourth."

"What's the fifth task?"

"I don't know, but the list is right there, so just read it." Jerry grabs the list, reads the fifth task, and then throws his head back in disbelief.

"Yo, my momma is tripping. She got me cleaning the bathroom."

"Just hurry up and do it, Jerry; you're wasting time." He grunts at Stacy's words as he heads to the bathroom.

Once he got in the bathroom, he stared at himself in the mirror for a bit. It wasn't long, though, because even though Jerry was popular and outspoken, he had quite a few insecurities. One of them was the way he looked. He thought his skin was too dark, his hair too nappy, and his lips too full. So the longer he stared in that mirror, it seemed as if he got darker, with bigger lips and no comb or brush in sight.

"Jerry, why are you just standing here procrastinating looking at yourself in the mirror?" Jerry continues to stare quietly.

"Jerry!" Stacy yells. He finally snaps back to reality.

"Huh?" Jerry said.

"Clean up. Why are you just standing there?"

"My bad."

"Yes, it is your bad; now hurry up."

Jerry loved how Stacy got on him about things, so he looked at her and smiled, saying, "Yes Ma'am." He started first with the sink, then the tub, and finally the toilet. He also swept and mopped the bathroom floor.

"Done!" Jerry says as he whips the sweat from his brow.

"Not quite," Stacy said, "you still have your room to clean, two loads of laundry to fold, and we still haven't started writing on that chapter novel your mother assigned to you."

"Oh yea, the novel," Jerry said with disgust, "well, I was speaking on just being done with cleaning the bathroom anyway."

"I know what you were trying to say Jerry, I was just pushing you to keep going until all tasks are done. There is no time for celebration."

Jerry loved her sense of urgency. It seemed as if she cared more about him not getting in trouble than he did for himself.

"You right Stacy, I'm about to get started folding."

"Yes, and while you fold, I'll read to you."

"Read to me?"

"Yes, read to you. I hope you didn't think I was just going to do it for you. What kind of girl do you think I am?"

"Well, I thought you were a good girl who liked doing homework, so I thought I was doing you a favor," Jerry said sarcastically.

"Really funny Jerry. A lot of jokes, but not a lot of sense. Shaking my head, just start folding."

"OK, OK," Jerry said, "let's get started."

As Stacy was reading, Jerry was folding as fast as he could. While he was folding, he noticed it was a little past three, which meant he had about thirty minutes left before Shelia Ann came walking through the front door. It made him a little nervous thinking about her arrival because he still had one more task to tackle which was cleaning his room.

As Stacy was reading, Jerry interrupted her saying, "Done!" Stacy paused from reading so that she could glance over at Jerry's work.

"Jerry, what in the world is that?"

"What do you mean? It's folded laundry."

"Ain't no way Jerry, that's how you fold clothes? That is absolutely ridiculous. I'm pretty sure that is going to make your mom more mad once she sees it."

"Maybe, maybe not, I don't know," Jerry says with his shoulders hunched and hands in the air, "but I gotta get started on my room, it's a real mess and I know that's the first thing she is going to check." Stacy rolls her eyes.

"OK Jerry, if you say, but I'm almost done reading and you might want to get started writing before your mom pulls up. Were you listening while I was reading?" Jerry just drops his head.

"Come on Jerry," Stacy said, sounding disappointed, "you have really got to do better. She only wanted you to read the first two chapters and then write a one-page paper on what it was about."

"OK well, I'm running out of time, so I have to pick one at this point, and I choose my room."

"Well, that's not a surprise to see you choose to labor over the lesson. You have to stop selling yourself short, Jerry. You have so much untapped potential, but it's on you to turn that energy kinetic."

"Labor over lesson? What does that even mean and what is kinetic?" Stacy blows a sigh of frustration.

"Just look it up Jerry; we don't have the time for me to sit here and break all of that down for you."

"All I was saying is what I've heard my grandfather say my entire life, which is don't be so quick to use your muscles over your mind."

"Now, let's get started on both."

"Both?"

"Yes, both. Find a pencil and a piece of paper. While you are sitting writing, I need for you to listen as I break down both chapters to you, then you can write in your own words. And also, as you are writing, I will be cleaning your room a little bit so that it won't look too bad once she arrives."

"OK, that sounds like a plan, I'm listening."

"OK, but before we get started, go ahead and open your window because when your mom pulls up and walks through that front door, I am out of here." Jerry laughs but agrees to Stacy's words.

So he immediately got up and opened the window as wide as he could so that Stacy could have a clear, quick, and clean getaway.

They made a great team. As Stacy was cleaning, she started to break down the novel to Jerry and as he was listening, he held tight to every word she spoke. He felt like, the way she was telling the story, why read? She should just narrate every time. He enjoyed the sound of her voice, no matter what she was talking about. Jerry was writing as fast as he could when all of a sudden, he heard another car door close. He and Stacy already had a foolproof plan ready to engage once Shelia Ann pulled up, but it didn't keep Jerry calm. His heart immediately started racing with sweat breaking from his stomach and from under his armpits.

"Aww man, mom's home. Stacy, you gotta go," Jerry said as he was walking to greet his mother at the door, but only to distract her from noticing Stacy climbing out the window.

"Wow, Jerry, you could at least help me out the window so I won't hurt myself." Jerry sprints back to the room.

"My bad Stacy, come on, I got you."

As he was helping her out of the window, she slipped and lost her footing for a second and fell back into Jerry's arms. Ironically, time seemed to slow down as they gazed into each other's eyes for a split second. After a brief moment of awkward silence, they both shook back to reality.

"You OK Stacy?"

"Yea, I'm good. Thanks for catching me."

"Naw, thank you for looking out today. You are the real MVP." Stacy giggles a little, but then they both hear keys jingling and the doorknob shaking.

"Bye, Jerry," Stacy says as she climbs down out of the window.

"Same time next week?" Jerry says sarcastically but a bit serious.

Stacy just continues to giggle and wave at Jerry as she walks back to her trailer.

"Junior!" Shelia Ann yells, "why does it smell like a little girl in my house?"

Of course, this left Jerry speechless. The only thing he could think of was the truth, but he knew that would send him to an early grave.

So he thought real hard about what he would and should say, then he looked up at his mother and said, "I don't know?"

CHAPTER 7

STACY CRIES WOLF

Stacy comes flying into the house, clenching her books tight to her chest. Her dad, Mr. Marvin, heard her running, but that didn't bother him. What did bother him was the sound of Stacy sniffing and sobbing as if she were crying. Then all of a sudden, he hears her door slam. The father in him just couldn't act like he didn't hear anything, so he hopped up and headed for Stacy's room. The closer he got to the door, the louder he could hear Stacy crying. Once he reached the door, he lightly knocked. He never wanted to seem like he was intruding on her space. TAP, TAP, TAP.

"Little Lady are you OK?" He hears nothing, so his actions become louder.

KNOCK, KNOCK, KNOCK, "Aht uhmm. What's wrong Little Lady?" He says as he clears his throat.

"Nothing Daddy, just girl stuff."

It really had everything to do with Jerry, but she didn't know how to talk to her dad when it came to other guys because he always got so defensive. He even made the statement one time that he didn't want her to even think about dating another guy until she was in her mid-thirties, close to forty. He was exaggerating, but that terrified Stacy. She figured that was too late and she would never find love waiting that long. So when it came to guys, she would always deflect.

"Are you sure? I mean, are you sure you don't wanna talk about it?"

"No Daddy, I'm fine, I promise."

"OK well, dinner will be ready in about an hour or so..."

"I'm not hungry!" Stacy says loudly through the door.

"I was just letting you know Little Lady, no need to yell at me. I love you," Mr. Marvin says as he walks away from the room door.

"Daddy, I wasn't…" Stacy sighs and shakes her head, "I love you too."

As she lay on her bed, she banged the back of her head continually against her pillow in frustration. How could Jerry think anything was going on between her and Ant? I mean, there was a very brief moment where Stacy did like Anthony, but there was never any action behind it. Ant never made a move, so Stacy just figured he didn't like her, or he was scared to ask. Either way, it didn't matter. She only had the heart eyes for Jerry, and it seemed like everyone knew and understood that except Jerry.

"He's always being so difficult," Stacy says to herself, *"and now I can't even see or talk to him at school tomorrow because he's always in trouble."*

"Ahhhh!" Stacy shouts, "I can't stand Jerry sometimes."

Stacy laid there until she fell asleep and slept well past dinner time. Once she had awakened, her stomach growled immediately. She checked her alarm clock and noticed it was four in the morning, which was way too early for her eyes to be open, so she forced herself back to sleep.

Stacy's alarm went off at 6:30 a.m. sharp. She usually didn't have a problem moving off the sound of her alarm, but this morning she hit the snooze button one time in order to roll over for just a few more minutes. Once her alarm sounded off again, she rolled out of bed.

Immediately, her thoughts revisited yesterday, but she shook those thoughts right out of her head and said, "OK girl, get it together."

She stood up, went to the bathroom, and then came back into her room and stood in front of her mirror attached to a wooden dresser her grandfather built for her with his bare hands. As she stared in the mirror, she played with her hair, trying to decide which style she was feeling today. First, the messy bun, but it was a little too messy. Then she tried braiding it but didn't feel like she had the time nor the patience to tangle with her hair, so she decided to grab her brush, hair gel, and edge control so that she could slick her hair back and show off that puff. After about four different outfit selections, she finally decided on a pair of blue high-waist jeans and a hot pink, long-sleeved Anime crop top. She had a few different options of lip gloss, but her favorite was the wild berry gloss with glitter. She threw on her pink and white Chuck Taylor's, and last but not least, a little less than half a roll of toilet tissue in order to stuff her bra. She didn't do it often, but occasionally. It was her sense of womanhood, even though she had a few years to go before she reached that point. One stage Stacy had reached in her young, innocent life was puberty and one of the things she hated most about it was acne.

"Ugh! How in the world do I wake up with a pimple the size of an ant hill on my forehead this morning," Stacy said with disgust, "where's my toothpaste."

She took the toothpaste and dabbed just a little on her index finger so she could cover her pimple while she finished getting ready. Her friend Tina told her about the toothpaste trick and she felt like Tina must have known what she was talking about because she didn't have any acne.

"Good morning Little Lady; how are you feeling today?"

Stacy always got dramatic with her father because she knew she had him wrapped around her pinky finger, so she looked at him with her eyes full of water.

"What's wrong Little Lady?" Mr. Marvin asked with concern.

"Daddy, my tummy hurts and I have a mountain top on my forehead which is making me feel like I need to change my hairstyle. I just really don't feel like going to school today."

"Well, Little Lady…"

"Daddy please, I'll clean up round here and have dinner ready when you get home from work today."

"As good as that sounds Little Lady, your education sounds better. I don't want you hanging round here taking care of me once I get old and crusty. I want you out in the world, putting yourself in the best position to be successful at all times. Life is all about choices, so choose wisely because failure never discriminates."

Stacy poked her bottom lip out, but she continued getting ready. She took heed to the things her father shared with her. He was a very smart man, and she admired him for that. As she was grabbing her bookbag and other handbag, she looked out of her window over to Jerry's and saw his mother in his room speaking with him. Shelia Ann was pointing her finger sternly at him, so Stacy suspected she was chastising him first thing in the morning.

"Poor Jerry," Stacy said, shaking her head, "I wonder what she could be getting on him about already." As she headed out the door, she told her father she loved him and gave him a kiss on the cheek.

"Love you too Little Lady, have a good day." Stacy headed down the dirt path smiling with Jerry on her mind.

"I really wish I had Jerry here to carry my books, but then again, he's never on time walking to the bus stop anyway," Stacy said to herself, laughing.

As she was walking, Shelia Ann came rolling past her heading to work. Stacy saw her out of the corner of her eye but she wouldn't turn her head. She just kept walking, which of course, didn't bother Shelia Ann at all. Stacy figured that maybe Jerry was still up since she saw his mother speaking with him this morning. So she texted Jerry but didn't get a response. She figured maybe he went back to sleep without any knowledge that his phone had been taken from him. Once she got on the bus, she was delighted to see her friends, but without Jerry on the bus, it felt empty. It felt as if the bus was moving with total silence and not even a soul operating the motor vehicle. She interacted with a few of her girlfriends but her focus was still on Jerry. After checking her phone a few times, she decided to call him. Again she got no response. At this point, she begins to get a little anxious because she knew she and Jerry didn't depart on the best terms yesterday, so she thought maybe he was ignoring her. After hearing Jerry's voicemail, Stacy got completely quiet, wrapping herself in her own thought process.

"Is Jerry really mad at me," Stacy thought to herself, *"like I know he sees me calling him."*

The more she got to school, the more upset she became because she still hadn't heard from Jerry. Even though they were not quite boyfriend and girlfriend, they still had an unspoken understanding and one of those understandings was to communicate in the morning. Whether it be by phone or the walk to the bus stop; either way, they made sure they heard each other's voice. The fact that it had not yet been done, threw Stacy's entire day off. From the moment she got off the bus, she had a bad attitude and was being short with anyone who spoke to her.

"Morning Stacy, hey Girl, come walk with us to breakfast!" a group of girls shouted as they exited their own bus.

Stacy rolled her eyes, kept walking, and acted as if she didn't hear them talking. It wasn't anything personal. She was just in her feelings for the moment and didn't want to be bothered by anyone or anything. As Tina got off the bus, she ran to catch up with Stacy.

"Girl, wait up! Why you moving so fast?"

"I'm just hungry. Ready to get to the café, that's all."

"Eww, the café! Girl stop lying; what's wrong with you, cause there must be something wrong if you rushing to the café. Don't nobody want no mystery meat."

"Tina, breakfast ain't even that bad," Stacy said, "it's lunch I gotta stay away from."

"Yea Girl, you right," Tina said as they both laughed.

As they sat and ate their breakfast, Stacy kept checking her phone for some type of response from Jerry.

"Stacy, why do you like Jerry so much?" Tina asked, "he's annoying and arrogant."

"No, he's sweet and funny," Stacy replied, "really, he's just misunderstood." Tina rolls her eyes.

"Whatever Girl, he just ain't my type."

As they walked to class after breakfast, she thought of calling him again, but she never wanted to seem desperate. So instead, she took a picture with Tina and sent it to him, but still no response. As she sat quietly to herself in her first block, she couldn't stay focused in class. It also seemed like the more she stressed out, the bigger her pimple got.

Stacy raises her hand abruptly and says, "Can I go to the bathroom please?"

The teacher granted her request, so she excused herself. Once she gets in the bathroom, she immediately checks her phone again, but still the same results.

"O.M.G! Is he really mad with me, like this doesn't make any sense." She didn't really have to use the bathroom, so she just washed her hands thoroughly while counting to 20 slowly.

"Gotta be germ-free," Stacy read out loud on the gossip wall as she turned the water off, *"probably the most positive thing I've ever read on the gossip wall,"* Stacy said to herself.

The gossip wall was where the sinks, mirrors, and soap dispensers hung, so as you were washing your hands, you could read about all the drama going on around the school. The gossip wall never discriminates. No one is safe. There seems to be breaking news on it every day, but you had to take in gossip wall information like a grain of salt, because it was 90% incorrect but 100% juicy. After grabbing a few paper towels, she dried her hands and tossed them in the trash. Then she made her way to the water fountain. As she gulped a few sips of water, she thought of ways she could get her dad to come get her from school early. She felt she wasn't in the correct headspace for school today. Then all of a sudden, a light bulb went off in her head.

"I know what to do, I'll call my dad and tell him my stomach is hurting. I know he will come and rescue me."

So that's exactly what she did. She went back into the bathroom, called her dad and begged him to come pick her up.

"Give me about an hour Little Lady, then I'll be there to get you."

"OK Daddy," Stacy said, smiling from ear to ear.

As she left the bathroom, she ran into the school counselor, Mrs. Warren.

"Hey Stacy, how have you been?"

"OK, I guess," Stacy replied.

"Why just OK?" Mrs. Warren asked.

"Well, it's this guy, and, well…"

"Ahh, boy problems, I see."

"Yes Ma'am."

"Well, one thing I can tell you about boys is they don't know what they want, so don't allow whatever they got going on to stall you or hold you back from becoming greater. You must move like time, understanding that you will leave others behind and that is OK. It is a part of life as we journey towards our destination." Stacy shakes her head in agreement.

"Thank you Mrs. Warren."

"You're welcome Stacy; continue to have a great day and remember, Kingdom Middle is better because you're here."

As Stacy completed her class work, she began to ponder some of the things Mrs. Warren spoke about and even though she was in full agreement about what she heard, it wasn't enough to change her mind about going home early. She had to face Jerry, and she was hoping that his mom would be at work so that they could talk without any distractions. The hour her dad promised her seemed like two. Finally, she heard her name over the intercom to report to the front office to sign out. She quickly grabbed her things and jetted out of the classroom. By the time she reached the office door, she had her sad face on so that her dad would feel bad for her.

"Aww Little Lady, are you OK?" Mr. Melvin asked with such concern.

"No, my tummy really really hurts Daddy. I don't even feel like I can stand up straight."

Stacy drops her things and flops into the seat next to her as if she is so weak. Miss Stevens wouldn't say a word at first. She just watched all of Stacy's theatrical movements and shook her head.

"Well Little Lady, do you think it could be that time of the month for you?" Stacy nodded her head yes.

"Well come on, that's nothing a little medicine and heating pad can't fix." Stacy smiled.

Her dad always knew what to say, so she gathered her things and followed behind him to the car. He opened the passenger door for her, as he always does. He took pride in being a complete gentleman for her. He would say things like, *"Stacy, if you can't find a guy to treat you or respect you the way that I do, don't allow them your time or attention. If they don't understand your worth, it must not be worth them understanding. You're the catch and not the chaser."*

As they drove down the road, Mr. Melvin asked Stacy if she was hungry and wanted to stop and grab a bite to eat.

"No Sir, I'm not hungry."

"Are you sure? Because I picked up an extra shift today at work, so I won't be home until late."

"I'm sure, I just want to lay down and get some rest. I feel like I'm starting to get a headache as well."

"OK, well, once we get to the house, I will go ahead and get the medicine and heating pad for you. I gotta move fast so that I can get back to work. My boss understood my emergency, but I don't wanna take advantage of her kindness."

As they pulled into the driveway, Stacy was looking down, but out of the corner of her eye, she noticed Jerry peeking through the blinds as her dad was assisting her out of the car.

"So I see he's not sleeping," Stacy thought to herself.

As they walked the steps into their house, Mr. Melvin was pretty much carrying Stacy through the threshold. Once they entered, Stacy headed straight for her room, and Mr. Melvin went straight to the kitchen cabinet. He grabbed the ibuprofen, shook out two tablets, and grabbed a bottle of room-temperature water. On his way, with the water and medicine, he grabbed the heating pad off the arm of the living room couch.

"Here you go Little Lady, I got you all set. Do you need anything else before I go?"

"No Daddy, I'm good," Stacy said with her face planted in her pillow.

"Alright, well, I'm about to get up outta here, I'll see you later this evening. Love you Little Lady!"

"I love you too Daddy. Finish having a good day."

The moment Stacy heard the front door close, she hopped up and went and stood by her window. She wanted to watch her dad pull off, but meanwhile doing so, she noticed Jerry looking from his bedroom window, watching her dad speed off hastily back to work. She also noticed a look in Jerry's eyes, as if he were upset about something. The moment she was sure her dad was out of plain sight, she burst out of the front door looking directly into Jerry's window. She saw that he acknowledged her with a head nod and a smile, which was enough to make her blush.

She couldn't be mad at Jerry for too long, so she just threw her hands on her hips with a slight smirk on her face saying, "Come here Jerry."

CHAPTER 8

SECRETS UNFOLD, TRUTH BE TOLD

"So you mean to tell me you don't know anything about this cheap, sweet smell in my house?"

Jerry replies back to her with a straight face saying, "No Ma'am, I really don't know where the smell came from."

"Uhumm, yeah OK, whatever Junior," Shelia Ann says in disbelief as she looks out through the kitchen window watching Stacy walk up the steps and into her own house.

"That little girl better not have been in my house Junior, especially without my knowledge."

"What are you talking about Ma? What little girl?" Jerry said, acting so confused.

"Don't play dumb with me. I can put two and two together. Why she ain't in school today? That little girl don't ever miss school, but on the day you sitting home, all of sudden, so is she. As a matter of fact, I drove past her walking down to the bus stop this morning. So I'm guessing she got out of school early today, huh?"

"Mama, I don't know."

"Stop lying; yes you do, but forget that right now. Did you get that list of chores done?"

"Yes, Ma'am, I was just finishing up writing now."

"Good, have it lying on my bed, ready for me to read once I get out of the shower."

"Yes Ma'am," Jerry replied. On her way to the bedroom, she stopped in the kitchen and looked around.

"My, my, Junior, those dishes sure are mighty clean and stacked up nicely to dry," Shelia Ann says as she observes the dish drainer.

"Well Ma, I learned from the best."

"Don't try to butter me up Junior."

"I'm not, I'm just saying…"

"And these floors are spotless, not a crumb in sight," Shelia Ann points out, "Jerry if I didn't know any better, I would've thought someone did your work for you."

Then she glanced over at the clothes piled on the couch, which were halfway folded and said, "Well, I mean, at least gave you a hand at it anyway."

"No Ma, I did it all myself." Shelia Ann just laughs hysterically.

"I'm sure you did Son. Imma take my shower, look over your work, and then get started on dinner. If you're not finished working by the time I get out, continue working on the paper until you finish while I cook."

"Yes Ma'am."

All Jerry had left in his paper to discuss was the conclusion. Stacy had already provided him with the introduction and body of work for the paper, so all he had to do was wrap it up. That didn't take him long at all, but it wasn't before he heard the water cut off from Shelia Ann's shower head.

"Junior!" Shelia Ann yells, "are you done yet?"

"Almost Ma," Jerry responds. While Shelia Ann was cooking, Jerry came into the kitchen smiling, gripping his paper tight.

"Oh, so you're finally done now, Junior?" Shelia Ann asked rhetorically.

"Yes Ma'am."

She snatches the paper and begins to read immediately. She read quietly as she made a variety of facial expressions. Jerry, again, was sweating around his stomach and under his armpits. He didn't know what was next after she got done reading, but then she started to nod her head up and down, eyes wide, with a frown on her face. Jerry stood there gazing at her with his mouth wide open.

"Wow Jerry, this is really good work. Good format and everything. I see you have an opening statement, introductory paragraph, body, and conclusion. Also, the paper is very detailed. This is outstanding Jerry, I'm very proud of you. Go get your clothes out for school tomorrow, take a shower, and come back out here for dinner."

"Yes Ma'am," Jerry says with a smile on his face. By the time Jerry had gotten out of the shower, he heard a knock on the door.

"Who is it?" Shelia Ann yells. There was no response, just another knock on the door.

"I said, who is it!"

"Shelia Ann, open the door," a deep voice replies.

"That better not be who I think it is," Shelia Ann says angrily as she walks toward the door.

"Well, that all depends on who you think it is," the deep voice replies.

"Don't play games with me, Jerry Sr., get away from my doorstep."

"Been a long time since I heard you say my name Shelia Ann and what a sweet sound it is. Brings back good memories."

"Well, that's good for you. Me, on the other hand, I have quite a bad taste in my mouth after saying your name."

"Come on now Shelia Ann, don't be like that. At least give me a chance to explain myself."

"There is nothing you could say to make up for what you did to this family."

"You're right, but there is plenty I can do from here on out to show you I've changed."

There was an awkward silence; then Jerry Jr. came out of the bathroom. Shelia Ann had her index finger over her lips and her other index finger pointing Jerry in the direction of his room. She didn't want Jerry Sr. to hear his voice.

"Junior, is that you?" Jerry Sr. asked, assuming it was because he heard footsteps and the bathroom door closing, "do you hear me Junior?"

Jerry Jr.'s eyes filled with water, but he doesn't respond to his father's call; he just wipes his eyes and closes his bedroom door. After a few more minutes of begging and pleading for Shelia Ann to open the door.

Jerry Sr. finally says, "Well, since you're not going to open the door, I'll sit out here and wait for you."

"Fine by me. We'll speak on my terms, not yours once you decide to pop up on some random night. Junior, come eat." As they sat there and ate, Shelia Ann made it a purpose to talk about anything but what was going on outside of her front door.

"Jerry, did you make sure you got your clothes out for school tomorrow like I asked you?"

"Yes Ma'am, I did," Jerry answered.

"Great, I want you to have a great day at school tomorrow. No goofing around and do as you are told."

"Yes Ma'am."

"And if you see that little Anthony boy, you act as if he doesn't exist. Do not speak to him, acknowledge anything he does, or play with him. Stay as far away from him as possible. I don't send you down to that schoolhouse to fight, I send you down there to learn, and that's what I expect for you to do. Understood?"

"Yes Ma'am," Jerry said with his head down, "Momma, why won't you let him in?"

"Jerry, that's nothing you need to worry about tonight."

"But Momma, what if he really does stay out there all night? He must've forgotten about how bad the mosquitoes were."

Shelia Ann laughed and said, "Well, they'll jog his memory. Now hurry up and finish eating. It's time for bed." Jerry did as he was told.

After he finished eating, he put his dishes in the sink and headed towards his bedroom. On his way, as he passed by the living room door, he tiptoed lightly and pressed his ear up against the door, hoping to hear his father make any kind of noise. He only heard creaks in the steps as he paced each one, mumbling under his breath and a few grunts. He wanted so badly to open the door, but first, he knew Shelia Ann would send him to an early grave, and second, he honestly did not know what emotion to feel or what emotion he should feel. Shelia Ann watched as pressed his ear against the door.

"Junior! Did you not understand what I said? I said goodnight."

Jerry drops his head and goes into his room, but he leaves the door cracked just in case Shelia Ann decides to open the door and let him in. Jerry wanted so badly to catch a glimpse of the voice behind the door. It has literally been years since Jerry saw his father, so with him being so close, just a few steps and closed door away, he felt he wouldn't get an ounce of sleep unless he at least put his eyes on him.

As the night grew later, it became harder and harder for Jerry to keep his eyes open. Even though he was curious and excited about seeing his father, the power of exhaustion had taken its toll. Every blink became a little heavier than the one before. Even though Jerry was home all day, that list of chores had him in motion for the entirety of it. His muscles relaxed; he blinked for the final time, then all of a sudden, 'BOOM'. Jerry hops up, runs to his room door and presses his shoulder against it as he peeks around the other side. What he saw caused his mouth to drop. The door was broken in and slung wide open. In comes a man with a hood over his head. Jerry could only assume it was his father since he was the only one sitting out on the steps, but he could only see a dark space inside the hoodie.

Shelia Ann screams, "Get out of my house! You are not welcome here!"

Jerry watches as his mother struggles with this man, who is clearly bigger and stronger than himself and his mother put together. He had all intentions of going over to help his mother, but he couldn't seem to take a step forward. He looked down only to notice both of his feet had been sunken into the ground. Jerry couldn't believe his eyes.

Then all of a sudden, he hears, "Junior! Please help, do something!" Shelia Ann shouts as she continues to struggle back and forth with this man.

Jerry looks back up, while in the same motion, the tall man with the hoodie on looks at him. I'm pretty sure the man could see fear all in Jerry's eyes, but on the other hand, Jerry couldn't see anything. All he saw was an empty dark space where the man's face should be. Jerry's heart dropped down into his stomach. He didn't understand why he couldn't make out any of this man's features. Not an eyebrow, a pair of lips, a nose, nothing. Jerry was more confused than scared at that point. The man drops Shelia Ann and heads straight toward Jerry. Jerry's heart begins to pound and his body shakes uncontrollably. He's drenched in sweat, clothes soaking wet. By the time the man with the hoodie approached him, he was completely speechless and frozen from shock.

"Leave us alone!" Jerry said in his head, but never out of his mouth.

The man with the hoodie grabbed Jerry by the shirt collar and lifted him out of the floorboards. The higher Jerry went, the wider his eyes got. He was terrified.

"Junior! Junior! Junior!" The man with the hood on kept repeating, but Jerry couldn't comprehend where his name was being called from because there was not a mouth, better yet, a face between the hood that the man was wearing.

"Junior!" The man shouts for a final time, "wake up!" Jerry wakes up in a puddle of sweat, eyes wide and full of water.

"Why are you crying and why are you wet?"

Jerry wouldn't say anything at first. He just stared at his father, observing every facial feature he couldn't make out in his dream, or nightmare rather.

"It's been a long time Son; get up and get yourself together. Your mother and I had a very long conversation last night and she agreed that I can drop you off to school this morning, but I wanna make sure it's OK with you first." Jerry didn't respond at first; he just kept staring in disbelief.

Shelia Ann, who was standing in the doorway, says, "Well, go on,

Junior, say something, don't be rude. You hear your daddy talking to you, don't you?"

A rush of energy begins to succumb to Jerry's emotions. He wasn't quite sure how to feel, but at the moment, he felt all of them. He was so happy to see his father but angry it took this long to see him again. He feared the reason why his dad left in the first place, but his curiosity built up enough courage and confidence to ask immediately.

"Where have you been?" Jerry Jr. asked, "and how come you never called or even stopped by to see me?" There was an awkward silence.

"Junior, just get yourself ready for school and I'll explain some things to you on the way there."

"OK," Jerry Jr. says as he hops out of bed to begin getting ready.

Before he got started, he dropped down to the floor in search of something under his bed. He crawled under and reached towards the back right corner and grabbed the six-pack his father had asked him to get out of the refrigerator many years ago.

"Here," Jerry Jr. said, "you may have to sit them back in the refrigerator." Jerry Sr. stares at the six-pack, only to keep from looking at Junior out of shame.

Jerry Sr. sniffs with his eyes full of water, clenching the six-pack with a tight grip, finally breaks the awkward silence, looks at Junior and says, "Son, I don't even drink anymore, but I got a brand-new tackle box, two spanking, brand new fishing rods, and a cooler full of drinks and snacks. The only thing I'll be missing is you and a bag of ice. So by the time I pick you up from school today, those drinks will be smothered in ice, and we'll be headed to the pond."

Jerry Jr.'s muscles in his face couldn't help but form a genuine grin. He was more than ecstatic to see his father and even more overwhelmed to know he would be spending the rest of the day with him, doing what he loved after school. Never before has Jerry gotten ready so quickly and prepared for school. Once he was done, Shelia Ann handed him his phone back and gave him a kiss on the cheek.

"Have a good day at school and remember all the things we discussed," Shelia Ann said.

"Yes Ma'am," he replied.

By the time Shelia Ann was done speaking with him, Jerry Sr. already had the engine running waiting on Junior. Jerry Jr. ran out, hopped in the truck, and immediately started comparing it to the old one.

"Oh wow, Pop, this is nice," Junior says as he looks around.

"Thanks Son, it's the same kind of truck from when you were younger, it's just a newer model."

"Oh OK, I'm guessing you stop smoking too, right?"

"As a matter of fact, I did," Jerry Sr. said with excitement, "what made you ask me that?"

"Because the old truck always smelled like smoke; even after you would clean it out, it still smelled like smoke."

"Yea, you're right, but that's nothing to worry about anymore. That's a thing of the past."

"Sure is Pop, amongst a lot of other things in the past."

"You right Son, I already know what you're getting at. There are many questions in the past that need answers, and I'm here to help you get those answers, so ask away. I will give you total honesty. That's the least I can do.”

Before Jerry Sr. could finish his statement, Junior quickly asked again, “Why did you leave and where did you go?”

CHAPTER 9

REUNITED

There was an awkward silence that fell over the car for about five minutes. It stemmed from Jerry Jr.'s questions that his father was already making seemingly hard to explain. Jerry Sr. puts his hand over his mouth, swallows spit, and clears his throat.

"Son, to be honest, there isn't a legit reason as to why I left. So as you are listening to me explain myself, know that I am not making any excuses for my shortcomings, I just want you to know and understand my state of mind during that time."

As Jerry Sr. began to explain himself, Junior couldn't stand to look at him as he was talking, so he just stared out the passenger window as he listened to his father talk.

"From the time your mother told me she was expecting your arrival into this world until around the time I exited your life, my expectations for what I needed to be for you were so high. The thing about those expectations was that they could never be satisfied. I could never do enough. For goodness sake, y'all are still in the same house I left you all in, and that's on me. It hurt my heart back when you were younger, those moments when you would ask me for a simple, cheap toy, a piece of candy, or a Happy Meal and I didn't have enough money to cover the spread. I was supposed to be your Superman, your Mario, your Hulk. It was and still is my job to protect and provide for you."

"I set these unrealistic goals that I was for sure a father is supposed to obtain, but really that couldn't be any further away from the truth. I had this whole idea in my head as to what a father is supposed to be for his child, so the moment one of those ideas did not line up, it seemed to spiral out of control, almost like a domino effect. All roads of disappointment led to me, and I couldn't bear the embarrassment of letting you and your mother down any longer."

As Senior spoke, Junior continued listening, but there was no emotion in his facial expression. He had the most blank, nonchalant look up on his face. He didn't respond to any of the information his dad was relaying to him at the time, he just kept staring out the window, but his vision began to blur as his eyes filled with water. As they turned into the school parking lot, Jerry Jr. would sniff and whip his eyes in order to keep his father and others from asking what's wrong. The moment the car stopped in front of the school, Jerry Jr. hopped out and ran inside without saying bye.

"Love you Son, I'll be right here waiting for you once you get out," Senior said as he watched Junior's backpack go up and down his back as he ran into the building.

"Stop right there young man," Principal Stewart said.

Now there were about three or four other young men that came in the building at the same time Jerry did, but Jerry had a hunch that the young man he was referring to was him.

"Yes Sir?"

"How was your day of O.S.S.? Were you productive?"

"Yes Sir, I was, my mother had an entire list of things for me to do and I had to have it all completed before she came in from work."

"Good," Principal Stewart said with a smile on his face, "I wish a lot more parents would have the same energy your mom did when their child faces O.S.S. The bad behavior around here would go down drastically. It starts at home. It always has, and it always will, but I also know that it takes a village to raise a child. That's where me and other teachers around here come into play. We are all here for each and every one of you. So maximize every resource available to you in order to help you reach your highest level of success."

"Yes Sir," Jerry said while nodding his head in agreement.

"Now get on to your class, have a great productive day, and remember your number counts here. It's never just another."

After those few words of assurance and encouragement, Jerry felt motivated and a little more confident in himself. As he entered class on time, which was considered rare for Jerry, his teacher Mr. Reid almost fell out of his seat in shock.

"Well, good morning to ya," Mr. Reid said, "It's great to see you bright and early; we missed you round here yesterday. Not gonna lie, the energy was 180 degrees without your presence, but nevertheless, your daily animation has its pros. More cons, I would say, but that is only because of the choices you decide to make after you take center stage of the classroom. Choose your words wisely, and also be more positive in your speech and actions."

Jerry was locked in on what Mr. Reid was sharing with him until Stacy entered the classroom. He immediately forgot Mr. Reid was even speaking.

"What's up Stacy!" Jerry said with a lot of enthusiasm.

"Hey Jerry," Stacy replied in a shy but cheerful way, "I never expected to see you this early."

"Yea I know, my dad dropped me off this morning," Jerry said pridefully, but he didn't understand why; his emotions were still all over the place.

"Your father dropped you off?!" Mr. Reid and Stacy said at the same time shockingly.

"Yes, he did and he said he is gonna pick me up from school today so that we can go fishing. I don't know if he thinks we will pick right back up from where we left off because there is a lot of work that has to be done in order to even get back where we were." Mr. Reid puts his arm around Jerry's shoulders and grips him firmly.

"I can relate to a lot of the things you are going through Jerry and if there is any advice you can take away from what I am about to share with you, please do. I grew up being bounced around from foster home to the next foster home. My mother was strung out on drugs, and my father a deadbeat. As I aged, I became more and more bitter, and I built a resentment towards my parents that I felt like they deserved. Now both of my parents are dead, and neither one of them ever truly knew how I felt. It doesn't matter if they would've truly cared or given an apology, it would have been just such a load off of my shoulders, but my pride let time slip right through my fingers. So sometimes you have to forgive people in order to free yourself. Allow your father the chance to right his wrongdoings."

"Oh wow Mr. Reid, that was deep. I got you, though. Thanks for that, I'm going to give my pops a real chance. I'm going to try to let the past remain in the past so that we can move forward."

"OK Jerry, I like the sound of that," Stacy said in agreement, "would you like to walk down to breakfast with me so we can eat before class?" Jerry was always down for some food.

"Yes Ma'am, I'm definitely down with that." They put their bookbags down by their assigned desk and headed out the door.

"Did your mom find anything suspicious with the work you did yesterday when she got home?" Stacy asked as they walked down the hallway. Jerry begins to sniff the air; then he starts to sniff around Stacy.

"As a matter of fact, she did find a few things suspicious, but she couldn't quite put her finger on it," Jerry said as he continued to sniff around her.

"Jerry stop, what are you doing, sniffing me like some dog."

"This is one of the suspicious things my mom couldn't put her finger on. Her exact words were, 'Who cheap, smelling perfume do I smell?'" Jerry repeated as he chuckled.

Stacy's mouth dropped.

"I know she didn't come for how I smell, I only wear the good stuff." Jerry continued to laugh.

"I'm sure you do. It smells good to me anyways so it's all good."

"You sure, 'cause the way you were laughing makes me feel like you're in agreement with your mom."

"Nah, I'm not, but I ain't gonna lie it was too funny when she said it. Honestly though, I was so nervous at the moment I couldn't even begin to smile. It wasn't until later that I thought about how funny it was."

"Yea, whatever Jerry, let's just change the subject because you're making me angry," Stacy says jokingly but a bit serious, "so, how were you feeling when you saw your dad? I could only imagine the thoughts in your head. Who spoke to who first? Did he make excuses, or did he apologize for being a no-good deadbeat?" Stacy's bombardment of questions only leads to a silent response from Jerry.

He didn't know how to answer her questions because it seemed as if he felt all the emotions at once when he saw his father, and his thoughts were racing faster than a prize horse; prep, trained, and ready for the Kentucky Derby.

"He spoke first," Jerry finally said after a few seconds of silence, "and no, he specifically said he was not making excuses, plus he also apologized and let me know his state of mind as to why he did what he did. He says we will talk more after school today once he picks me up to go fishing. Just me and him, but I don't know if I want to reminisce on the past. It might ruin a good moment. I've missed him so much, so just his presence down by the pond means everything to me. I miss watching his fingers as they would fiddle through the tackle box looking for something that he would never seem to find. As I would shake my head and laugh, pops would always say 'Oh well, guess it wasn't that important if I left it,' but the thing is I never knew what he was looking for or what it was that he left behind, other than me and my mom of course," Jerry said sarcastically.

"Wow Jerry, what a very dark sense of humor you have," Stacy replied.

"Yea well, you know what they say, laughter is the best medicine."

"I don't exactly agree with that," Stacy said with her head tilted, "I do believe laughter is good medicine for the heart, but I do not believe it is the best. My dad says laughter is more like Tylenol or ibuprofen, it just numbs the pain, its primary job is not to heal. Laughter is nothing more than a quick fix to your problems, a deflection to your struggles. Daddy says that understanding and having awareness of yourself and things around you is real medicine. That's it! That's the cure. Being able to evaluate yourself unbiased and problem solve the challenges in your personal situation."

"Wow, that might actually be one of the deepest, smartest, and most definitely different perspectives I have ever heard on laughter. Makes me wanna tighten up and take life more seriously," Jerry said jokingly but he heard every word she said as they stood in line patiently awaiting breakfast.

After they ate breakfast, they headed back for their homeroom class, which was with Mr. Reid. Jerry and Mr. Reid had already gotten off to a great start this morning, and Jerry had plans of keeping it that way. He was on time, actively working on his morning class work, and he made it a point not to go back and forth with Mr. Reid. Once the first period ended, he made sure he wasn't anywhere near the back of the line, because he already knew how Miss Sanchez was when it comes to tardiness. She doesn't play. Without that tardy slip, it's an automatic write-up. He didn't make his way to the very front of the line, but he was near the front so it was good enough.

"Good morning Miss Sanchez," Jerry said eagerly, "look, see I'm on time Miss Sanchez!"

"Buenos Dias Jerry," she replied, "I'm so glad to see you here and on time. Now let's keep the ball rolling and stay focused on our work today and be very attentive."

"Yes Ma'am," Jerry said as he had a seat.

Not only would Jerry remain focused and attentive throughout the rest of the day, but he would also find himself being overly helpful today. He held the door for anyone walking behind him, allowed ladies to go first ahead of him in the lunch line, and he also helped two people pick their books up off the floor as he was walking down the hallway. He was the definition of a good Samaritan. He wasn't quite sure what it was that had him feeling the way he was feeling. He didn't think seeing his dad would have this type of impact, but he for sure did not want to give his dad all the credit for the type of day he was having. Or was he deserving of it? Jerry always had it in him to do what's right; he just lacked motivation. Once his dad left when he was in the second grade, he slipped into a dark, rebellious state, but now that his father is back, he is starting to feel a sense of joy that he hasn't felt in a long time.

CHAPTER 10

JUST LIKE OLD TIMES

Well, the last bell of the day finally rang. Immediately after, all car riders were called down to the front in order to wait for their rides. Before Jerry could get outside, he saw his father's truck from a distance. It could have been his imagination, but he also felt like he heard his dad's roaring engine and tailpipes through the school walls. His anticipation caused him to start sweating all over, and his emotions had no guidance. Before he knew it, he was running full speed, breathing heavily on his way to the car.

"Slow down Jerry, walk! My goodness Son, you ran in here this morning now you running out. The rules haven't changed Jerry, so act accordingly."

"Yes Sir," Jerry said as he walked hastily past Principal Stewart, "see you Monday." As Jerry entered the truck, he noticed it was loaded down for fishing, just like his dad said.

"Hey Son, how was school?" Jerry Jr. eyes began to swell with water; he couldn't even remember the last time his dad asked him that.

"It was good," Jerry said with a smile on his face.

"Ok, that's great," Jerry Sr. replied, "you ready to cast a new rod?" Jerry Jr. couldn't stop smiling.

"You betcha."

As Jerry Jr. hopped in the truck, it seemed as if he and his father picked right up from where they left off in the second grade. Jerry Sr. began to drop knowledge on him like he used to and make comparisons of life to fishing.

"Were you the fisherman or the fish today?" Jerry Sr. asked.

"Huh?" Junior replied.

"Were you the fisherman or the fish?" Jerry Sr. repeated.

"I don't think I get what you are asking," Junior said, but seemingly over curious to find out.

"What I mean by asking you if you are the fisherman; are you the one baiting, manipulating, misleading or tricking? Or, are you the fish? Which means you're easily baited, manipulated, or misled."

Jerry Jr. thought hard but didn't have a response. It seemed cruel to explain a fisherman in that light, but he thought to himself *that he definitely wasn't a fish*.

"Neither," Junior said confusingly.

"Good answer, never tempt others and most definitely don't be so easily tempted. Your mother shared with me that it has been a rough week for you in school."

"Yea," Junior replied.

"Yea!" Jerry Sr. said with his eyes wide and eyebrows raised.

"Oh, I most definitely have been gone too long. What happened to yes and no sir?"

Jerry Jr. looked his father straight in the eyes and said, "What happened to you saying goodbye the day you left or what happened to at least a phone call from time to time or something. SOMETHING! Something that would let me know you still cared, loved, and wanted me. Something to let me know you were even still alive. I mean, did you care to even know if I was living or not? Did you lose as much sleep as I did wondering when I would see you again or if I even would?"

Jerry Sr. didn't say a word as he allowed his son to vent. Junior went on and on about a few different things he mentally oppressed over the years, and as he released, Jerry Sr. began to sweat from embarrassment. His palms were so wet he could barely grip the steering wheel as he drove. Once Jerry Jr. was finished speaking, there was an extended silence inside of the car. That silence lasted all the way to their destination. Junior's silence came from exhaustion, pain, and anger, so he just stared out the passenger window, but Senior's silence came from a place of empathy and reflection. He took in every word given to him by his son and thought deeply about it. In order to break the awkward silence as they exited the car, Jerry Sr. gave out instructions.

"I got the rods Son. Can you grab the tackle box and…."

"Yea, yea, and the other side of the cooler. I got it," Jerry Jr. said ever so nonchalantly, "it's been a long time, but I haven't forgotten."

"Junior, if you don't want to fish, we don't have to. It seems like I've angered you enough for today. Do we need to just hop in the truck and head on home?" Jerry Jr. wouldn't respond, he just looked down and kicked the dirt with his hands in his pockets.

"Son, do you hear me talking to you?"

"Stop calling me that. Stop talking to me like everything is as normal as it used to be. Did you think after your speech this morning, everything would be fine, forgotten, and forgiven? I'm more confused now than I've ever been with even more questions. My main one is, why now? After all these years, you popped up last night. What do you want, why are you really here, and have you been missing me any of the time you were gone or was it just all of a sudden? I missed you every day Pop, and I thought about you every second," Jerry Jr. said as he began to cry, "every thought I had come with different feelings."

The thought of Jerry and his father spending time together made him happy for what he missed, but the thought of them spending time together also made him sad for what he was missing. The image of his father's taillights dimming as he drove into the distance still plays on repeat in his head, which causes him to feel anger and frustration.

"For a long time, I felt like I was the reason you drove off so fast. Some days I feel like I still am. Maybe if I hadn't asked you to go fishing so much or not always asking for something to eat, then maybe you would've stuck around a little longer. I'm sorry…"

"No Son, I'm sorry, I'm so, so sorry," Jerry Sr. said with much compassion in his voice, "you don't owe me any apology for being a kid, I've let you down so many times and I'm realizing that every day I made the choice not to come and see you, it was letting you down over and over again. Son, I mean Junior, I vow to you my loyalty, time, effort, and understanding. I know it will take time for us to even come close to where we used to be, but I'm here for you every step of the way if you allow me. I'm not asking you to forget the past, I'm asking you to forgive it." Junior nodded his head up and down while grabbing the other side of the cooler.

"OK Pop, I'm willing to give it a try. Now we better hurry up and get down by the pond, those fish ain't gonna catch themselves."

As they walked the trail down to the pond, they both began reminiscing on the times when they fished together. Jerry Jr. would remind him of things that Senior had almost forgotten.

He would outburst with laughter and say things like, "Wow, that did happen," or "I can't believe you still remember that."

They fished for about an hour and a half. After fishing, they went and got ice cream just like they used to. They both enjoyed the same flavor of ice cream, Cookies-N-Cream. Things seemed like they were really starting to shake back into place. Once they finished with their ice cream, they stopped by a local park because they saw a group of Little League baseball players getting ready to play. Before they hopped out of the car, Jerry Jr. was overwhelmed with joy.

"OOO…Pop, I love baseball, I can't wait until I start playing."

"Your mother told me you missed tryouts because of decisions that you made leading up to that point. Is that true?"

"Yes Sir," Jerry Jr. said with his head down.

"What did I tell you about looking down? Wrong or right, you make eye contact with whoever is speaking." Once Junior looked up and made eye contact, then Senior started back speaking.

"Saying what you want is the equivalent of potential energy. For instance, great ideas and suggestions with no plan of execution behind it. Kinetic energy is turning all those great ideas or suggestions from a stand still motion into action. Son you have to say what you mean, and also be able to follow through with it. Too many people let themselves down with unrealistic goals or broken promises. Don't be like me when it comes to that. You are better, so do and act accordingly." Jerry Jr. began to smirk with a slight grin when he thought about what his father was saying.

He thought to himself, *"Pop is right, I am better. I would never do some of the things he did when I'm all grown up."* The game was getting good, but they both had food on their mind.

"Well Son, we've been hanging out all evening. It's about time I get you to the house. I know your mother is done with dinner by now, plus I can taste that sweet strawberry tea on the tip of my tongue. I bet it's still the best in the neighborhood."

"You know it Pop, if there is competition, I ain't seen or heard of it," Junior said as they both laughed.

"It's like your mother mixes the perfect amount of strawberries with just the right amount of sugar, and what about those biscuits Son? Are they still the golden standard?" Senior asked.

"Yes Sir. She has gotten better at making them since you left, too Pop. She be making strawberry and blueberry butter biscuits as well."

"No, she don't, do she?" Senior asked as his mouth watered and his stomach growled.

"Yes indeed she does. You right Pop; it's about that time. The more and more we talk about it, the hungrier I get." They walked to the truck hastily and hopped in with great anticipation of Shelia Ann's cooking.

During the ride home, Junior told his dad about the speaker his mom had gotten him at the yard sale. He spoke about the different instrumentals saved to his playlist and how he could imitate them. He proved to his father how good of a beatboxer he was, and Senior was truly impressed. He not only noticed that his son had a talent but that he had turned it into a skill.

"Wow Son, you nice with it," Senior said as he bobbed his head, "you really have a gift, but the coolest part about it is that you're manifesting it."

As they drove into the driveway, both of them could see Shelia Ann through the kitchen window, setting the dinner table. With excitement, they jumped out of the truck and ran into the house. They were immediately halted by the sight and smell of the dinner table. Of course, at the center of it were the homemade butter biscuits and that freshly made strawberry tea.

"Dinner time Boys, wash your hands and say your grace before you eat," Shelia Ann said with pleasure.

It was something about her saying that seemed to bring a family connection between the three of them. It looked right, sounded right, felt right, and to Jerry Jr., it was right. Things were nowhere near perfect, but for Jerry Jr., this was a great start.

ABOUT THE AUTHOR

CarolinaKidd

I was born May 21, 1992, in Frankfort, Germany. The reason is that my father was a soldier in the U.S. Army. I was only thereafter my birth for approximately two years, and then my parents and I headed for the States.

As I began to age, basketball became my favorite pastime. At times, I felt as if I loved the game more than it loved me; I still persevered through trial and error, and I now withhold memories, moments, mistakes, and accomplishments from the game that I share with young men and women. Hopefully, my past will make brighter futures for the young minds I instill.

Poetry is my second favorite pastime, right after basketball. I always took an interest in rhythm, rhyme, and patterns, but I never did pick up a pen and start writing until 2008, when my mother passed away. I did not know I had it in me, but for some reason, that was the only way my mind would release negative energy. I could not stop writing once I started, and I have not looked back since. **"Where is She"** is the first poem I ever wrote. I cried as I wrote the piece, only thinking of my deceased mother, but little did I know the power of poetry rose within me.